# IT WAS "THE-WORST-THING-YOU-HAVE-EVER-DONE" GAME— WITH A DEADLY NEW TWIST

In the daybreak hours of a cold gray December 4, 1995, police were called to a shocking murder scene not far from Dallas. Blond, green-eyed Mansfield High School sophomore Adrianne Jones had been brutally bludgeoned and shot in the face. Authorities quickly narrowed their list of suspects—but as months ticked by, the grisly murder went unsolved.

David Graham was in tears at Adrianne's funeral. And he and Diane Zamora attended a candlelight vigil held in Adrianne's behalf. Along with other friends of the murdered girl, they held hands, sang songs, and prayed for the capture of whoever was responsible for this horrible crime.

It wasn't until the following July that Diane, playing "the-worst-thing-you-have-ever-done" game with fellow plebes at the Naval Academy, topped them all with: "My boyfriend and I murdered a girl back in Texas." And soon detectives were piecing together a shocking story of forbidden passion and blood vengeance. . . .

# THE CADET MURDER CASE

# THE CADET MURDER CASE

## A True Story of Teen Love and Deadly Revenge

## A. W. Gray

AN ONYX BOOK

ONYX
Published by the Penguin Group
Penguin Books USA Inc., 375 Hudson Street,
New York, New York 10014, U.S.A.
Penguin Books Ltd, 27 Wrights Lane,
London W8 5TZ, England
Penguin Books Australia Ltd,
Ringwood, Victoria, Australia
Penguin Books Canada Ltd, 10 Alcorn Avenue,
Toronto, Ontario, Canada M4V 3B2
Penguin Books (N.Z.) Ltd, 182–190 Wairau Road,
Auckland 10, New Zealand

Penguin Books Ltd, Registered Offices:
Harmondsworth, Middlesex, England

Published by Onyx, an imprint of Dutton Signet,
a division of Penguin Books USA Inc.

First Printing, April, 1997
10  9  8  7  6  5  4  3  2  1

to America's teens

# THE CADET
# MURDER CASE

# Prologue

At six-thirty the morning of December 4, 1995, Gary Lynn Foster rose for another day at work. A broad-shouldered man of medium height, Foster lives on isolated property a mile and a half west of Joe Pool Lake. He's a man who likes his privacy. He fixed and ate his breakfast, enjoyed the pleasant weather of that winter while drinking a cup of coffee on his porch, then climbed in his pickup and headed for work as the sun came up.

Foster's home is a sturdy red brick two-story set far back from Seeton Road, the winding blacktop thoroughfare leading from Mansfield, Texas, out to the lake. The house is barely visible from the road; later, reporters visiting the scene were to assume that the property was vacant except for a few sagging outbuildings. It's a bumpy 150-yard ride down a dirt driveway from the house to Seeton Road. A row of rusty, bashed-in U.S. Postal boxes are set across the street from Foster's property, and that is where he gets his mail. Foster stopped his truck and reached inside his box to see if he had anything. As he leaned out, something fluttering in the breeze caught his eye.

Across the road, not thirty feet from the mailboxes, is a waist-high barbed-wire fence on both sides of a cattle guard. Twenty yards beyond the fence are two ramshackle old buildings that look like henhouses. The buildings border a clearing enclosed by rows of elm trees, and on the other side of the trees is a large field dotted with cylindrical bales of hay. The fluttery motion that had caught Foster's eye was a strip of cloth hanging on one of the fence barbs. It held Foster's attention for only a fraction of a second. Then he saw in the clearing between the fence and the trees, a body lying on the ground.

Foster's initial reaction was one of irritation. The lonely stretch of blacktop in front of Foster's place is one of the local high school kids' favorite hell-raising haunts, and Foster had been awakened more than once by the screech of burning rubber on asphalt or the tinkling sound of shattering glass. He was sick and tired of cleaning broken beer and whiskey bottles from in front of his hay fields, and all he needed now was a leftover from last night's partying, passed out drunk on his property. To the left of the cattle guard, the barbed wire was trampled and bent. He got out of his truck and walked over to the fence.

He neared the fence and squinted in the early morning light for a better look. The figure on the ground was a girl, wearing flannel shorts and a long-sleeve knit pullover. She was on her back, her slim athletic legs spread, her arms flung out on either side. She had fluffy blond hair, wore no shoes, and had painted toenails.

Foster called out to the girl. When she didn't move, he walked a few paces to his left and started to enter the field via the cattle guard. As he did, he had a side-slant view from a different angle than he'd seen from the road. Foster backed away and gagged.

There were two gaping holes in the girl's head. Each wound was twice the size of a silver dollar, one through her temple and one through her cheekbone. Both holes were filled with thick, coagulated blood. Her skull was caved in, and visible through whitish bone was a gray substance that Foster was certain was brain matter. He turned his back, bent from the waist, and covered his eyes.

In a few seconds his vision cleared, and he stood erect. He wasn't about to approach the corpse—or, for that matter, to look at the grisly spectre a second time—and as his revulsion slowly subsided, he felt a pang of fear. He was all alone out there with a brutally murdered girl not ten steps away, and for all he knew her killer was hiding behind the nearest tree, ready to do him in as well.

His head throbbing, Foster ran to his truck, gunned the engine, and roared back down Seeton Road. He reached his driveway, reversed gears, then didn't let up on the accelerator until he'd reached his doorstep. Trembling, he staggered into his kitchen and picked up the phone to call the police.

# 1

Though Mansfield, Texas, lies only twenty miles from Dallas' mirror-walled highrises and New-York-minute lifestyle, until recently most Big D residents had never heard of the place. And little wonder. Interstate 20, the main artery leading to Abilene and points west, skirts a good ten miles north of Mansfield, and Highway 67, the southeast four-laner to Midlothian and Cleburne, bypasses it a like distance to the south, so no matter where you're going you don't pass through Mansfield on the way. It was "down a piece" from Grand Prairie, a "hoot 'n' a holler" from Cedar Hill, and a "nice Sunday drive southeast of Fort Worth if a body's got a hankering for something countryfied."

Pretty country it is. The surrounding area is a pleasant expanse of sweet-smelling cedars and thick-limbed elms that sprout from some of the blackest, richest land in all of Texas. It was this that prompted settlers, hardy Scotch-Irish folk, to battle Kiowa and Comanche and establish a sawmill on Walnut Creek in the late 1840s. A pair of speculators named Julian Feild and Ralph Man bought up 540 acres in 1856 where they built the first steam-operated grist mill in the Southwest. The Man-Feild Mill prospered during the Civil War, and delivered flour and cornmeal to the Confederacy as far away as Shreveport and Jefferson City, Missouri. Likely it rankles Julian Feild's descendants that the town was incorporated in 1890 as "Mansfield," but what the heck, Texans of the day were not much into spelling anyhow.

The growth spurts of the twentieth century, particularly in Dallas and Fort Worth, bypassed Mansfield altogether. In 1951 the Mansfield directory listed only 432 names, and the population didn't reach a thousand until the 1960 census. Through the sixties and seventies, Mansfield continued to slumber. Kids joined groups like Future Farmers of America and those sponsored by the Church of Christ, raising prize livestock to haul to the state fair. As the 80's dawned, however, things were about to change.

It took awhile for the inner-city wars that plagued L.A., New York, and Chicago to invade Dallas, but by the eighties the malaise was well underway. Combined with federal ruling on school busing and red-lining of residential districts, these changes caused many residents to look for housing elsewhere. As the seventies came to an end, bedroom commuter communities thrived in the mid-cities of Irving, Grand Prairie, and Arlington, and in the northern Dallas-area towns of McKinney and Plano. I-45, I-30, and Highway 183 became bumper-to-bumper morning and evening.

None of this affected sleepy little Mansfield, or its neighboring townships of Cedar Hill and Midlothian, until the developers zeroed in on the large, uninhabited, forest-covered area south of Grand Prairie and noted the potential there. Although lacking highway access, Greater Mansfield was nonetheless a prospective gold mine if the developers could add the right attraction. In landlocked North Central Texas the right attraction is a lake.

The setting had been in place for centuries. The low hills to the south form a natural valley. Walnut and Lynn creeks, along with the John Penn and Baggett branches of the Trinity River, flow to the north, away from the Gulf of Mexico, and damming the northern rim of the valley would create an impressive body of water. But construction of a dam anywhere in the United States is a massive undertaking. There is bureaucratic red tape in securing permits, millions upon millions of tax dollars to be raised, contractors to be hired, and quasi-government river authorities to be organized. One of the more common methods of assuring success is to name the lake after the politician whom developers need in their corner; Lake LBJ near Austin is a prime example of such maneuvering, though the entire state of Texas is dotted with bodies of water named for elected officials of whom most people have never heard.

Joe Pool Lake was named after the congressman from the Oak Cliff section of Dallas, which included Mansfield in his constituency. He died in the late seventies while the lake was still on the drawing board. The lake opened in 1988, and with it brought the subdivisions, golf courses, and a surge in population. Modern gated communities quickly surrounded the shores of the lake, and sailboats and motor-driven yachts appeared on the water. From a hamlet of 3,600 in 1970, Mansfield grew by 1995 to over 21,000, and the forecast is that more than 50,000 will live in Mansfield by the early twenty-first century.

There are growing pains. While the residents of the new subdivisions sport Mansfield addresses, pay taxes, and give to local charities, they are transplanted city dwellers. They spend a great deal of their time "en route," driving back and forth to Dallas to work. There's a new modern high school; whereas Mansfield kids formerly arrived for classes in yellow buses, wearing overalls or hand-me-downs from older siblings, the high school parking lot is now filled with shiny sports cars and the kids come to school in Polo and Tommy Hilfiger labels. The hayrides of yesteryear are history. Nineties Mansfield teenagers go on dates into the city, stroll the West End, and dance the Macarena at Deep Ellum nightspots.

Mobility has brought a close to Mansfield's age of innocence. There are freakers in Mansfield, kids with half-shaved heads and faces made up like Halloween. Violent crime is on the upswing. Unthinkable acts on the part of teenagers, commonplace in cities for decades, have now arrived in Mansfield; the little city reeled in shock when a lovely sixteen-year-old named Marie Robards poisoned her father's refried beans with barium acetate from high school chemistry class, hid the crime for nearly a year, then confessed to a friend as they rehearsed for senior class production of *Hamlet*. Marie's parents had divorced in 1980; in her confession to police, she stated that she killed her father because she wanted to live with her mother.

Reality blasted home to the community once again, however, in the wee morning hours of December 4, 1995, when on a lonely road near Joe Pool Lake, persons unknown bashed in the skull of a pretty sixteen-year-old, chased her into a nearby field, shot her twice in the face, and left her dead. The girl's brutal murder and its after-

math kindled shock waves that ultimately rever-
berated through the entire nation, and bore final
proof that the sleepy town of Mansfield, Texas,
will never be the same again.

# 2

They would remember her best as a pretty girl who loved to run, and who in time would have been a lovely woman. Already as a high school sophomore she was turning heads as she jogged through Mansfield streets on her way to and from school or work, chin held high, wealth of blond hair bobbing around her shoulders.

Along with the rest of her peers she was, in her own mind, invincible. The warnings of parents, teachers, television personalities in community service ads, and police department reps at school assemblies—*drive carefully, practice safe sex, don't stay out too late, steer clear of drugs*—went in one of her ears and out the other because she couldn't believe any of that *bad stuff* could ever really happen to her.

Adrianne Jones spent the last sunny December Sunday afternoon working at Golden Fried Chicken, where she was a part-time employee. A pretty girl, she was a major asset to the tiny fast-food place on Broad Street near the town square. She was also a dependable worker and a natural born salesperson brimming with enthusiasm.

Golden Fried Chicken, a remodeled fifties drive-in, is just down the road from an elementary school, and doesn't have much drop-in business. The standard take-out eateries—McDonald's and Wendy's, Taco Bell and Taco Bueno, Pizza Hut and Pizza Inn—are out on the 287 bypass, servicing the new upscale subdivisions.

All of this translates to lots of down time for GFC employees. Adrianne would have no part of being bored, though. Her pick-me-up devices ranged from kid stuff—firing spit wads at her coworkers through drinking straws, doing her impression of Michael Jackson's moonwalk as she performed her table-busing duties—to playing mother confessor to other employees, lending a sympathetic ear to their personal problems, pouring out some heartfelt tidbits of her own. Tina Dollar, the all-business young woman who continues to manage the Golden Fried Chicken today, held her irritation in check at most of Adrianne's antics because the pretty teenager was good for business. Even when Adrianne spent a bit too much time on the phone with her friends, Tina looked the other way.

Adrianne never lacked for boyfriends. She had even, honest features, her slightly crooked front teeth adding to her full-of-mischief grin. As a child she'd tended on the chubby side, but ever since she'd found athletics as a seventh-grader she'd been racehorse trim. Running shoes seemed her only footwear; otherwise, summer and winter alike, Adrianne preferred to go barefoot. She'd been a potential soccer star, leading her junior team to the city finals, but a knee injury during her freshman high school year had relegated her to sideline duty as the team manager. The bum knee limited only her ability to cut, to change direction in midstride, and so she switched from soccer to track and cross-country. She stayed in tiptop shape. Boys—and older men as well—noticed, and Adrianne enjoyed the attention.

She worked because she had to. Her dad labored as a heavy machinery mechanic, and her mother gave massages at a beauty salon. Adrianne had to make her own spending money. The Golden Fried Chicken wasn't her first employer—it was her third—what little earnings she could save rested inside a red metal mailbox in her bedroom. She dreamed of going to college, but whether she ever would have made it is a toss-up. Adrianne, like most teenagers, was a bit of a spendthrift; her most recent splurge was a series of poses from Glamour Shots, which she planned to distribute as Christmas presents. The photos would come in the mail on the day after Adrianne died.

The weather was oddly springlike for December 3. The thermometer touched seventy degrees in mid-afternoon, and there wasn't a cloud visible anywhere. Yet the afternoon shift at the Golden Fried Chicken was even deader than normal because, thirty miles to the north, the Cowboys were playing at home at Texas Stadium. What happens to the Dallas-Fort Worth metroplex during Cowboy games is a phenomenon; the metropolitan area of three and a half million becomes a giant ghost town as its citizens crowd into stadium seats or huddle around television sets in living rooms or rowdy bars. Grown men paint their faces silver and blue and whoop like Sioux in bloodlust. Malls are deserted, clerks staring through display windows at nothing.

Adrianne wasn't much of a football fan. Occasionally the fry cooks would cheer or groan over the portable black-and-white back in the kitchen, and Adrianne would ask the score—more to be with-it than from any real curiosity, for any North Central Texan who doesn't live and die with the Cowboys' fate is considered a ninny. Mainly, though, she stayed on the phone, laying the receiver down only to wait on infrequent drive-through customers. No one asked her to identify her callers, but it was apparent that she was making plans for later on.

"Later on" in Adrianne's world meant the wee hours of the night after adults had gone to bed. Adrianne was part of a group of kids who thought the fun didn't really begin until after midnight. For the past couple of years she'd crept out of the house late at night on a regular basis, more often than not in the company of older boys, experimenting with sex and drugs, prowling the streets of Mansfield and the back roads near Joe Pool Lake until the crack of dawn. She'd been careless of late, for her father recently had discovered her forays and had nailed down her bedroom windows. Yet this would not keep Adrianne home after hours. She was, after all, invincible. Bad things had happened to a good friend of hers, but she hadn't drawn any lessons from it. Those were the sorts of things that only happened to other people.

### Close-up

"Nobody really got in trouble or anything," the teenage girl says. "We were just, you know, tripping." Her name is Heather Reed. She works full-time at Burger King, having dropped out of Mansfield High two months prior to graduation.

"You don't call what happened to Adrianne Jones 'getting in trouble'?" the interviewer says.

She blinks guardedly. "Well, except for that."

"I don't see how you could make it to school, staying out all night," the interviewer says.

"Wasn't *every* night." She seems thoughtful. "Three or four times a week is all."

"But you did miss some school?"

"Yeah, some. You see where I'm working now." She laughs quickly, then her smile fades.

"You see Adrianne out at night quite a bit?"

"Some. Not as much as a lot of us. More than some others."

"That's when the kids around here did most of their drugs?"

"Not all of them," she says. "Some after school, around. But, yeah, late at night, a lot of it."

"All you kids sneaking around all night . . . didn't your parents catch on?"

She shrugs and brushes a wisp of hair off her forehead. "My dad lives in Minnesota. My mom, she works. After about ten at night she's just dead."

"Never wakes up and wanders around the house?"

"If she does, I don't know about it."

"What about after what happened to Adrianne? Did that slow down the nighttime activities any?"

She blinks. "She was messing with somebody else's boyfriend, you know."

"And you think that's an excuse for someone killing her?"

"It's something you don't do," she says. "You can get hurt over it."

16

"This is all foreign to me. Suppose I'm older, but . . . are you saying that girls physically attacking other girls over their boyfriends, it's a common occurrence?"

"Happens all the time, mister."

"Like with Kimberly Horton?"

She grins. "You know about Kim and that thing?"

"I've heard some. Maybe you can fill me in."

"Kimmy got the shit beat out of her."

"Wasn't she Adrianne's best friend?"

"I don't know about *best* friend," she says. "But they ran around a lot."

"Enough so that Adrianne would have known what happened to Kimberly?"

"Sure, she testified in court, at Lindsay's probation hearing."

"Lindsay?"

"The girl that done it."

"Beat Kimberly up?" the interviewer asks.

Heather nods, and looks at the clock on the far wall. From his station behind the serving counter, the Burger King manager watches her. "Happened a long time ago, when we were all about fourteen."

"What did Kimberly do to get in trouble?"

"I told you. She was slipping out with Lindsay's boyfriend and, you know, doing it with him."

"Having sex?"

17

"Sure, yeah. Doing drugs, too."

The interviewer sighs. "Fourteen years old."

"The guy was older. Sixteen, I think."

"So she was carrying on with Lindsay's boyfriend. How did Lindsay find out?"

"The guy told her."

"Sounds similar to what happened with Adrianne," the interviewer says. "Why do you think, if he was messing around, he'd tell his girl-friend?"

"Sometimes these guys get off on it. Want to, you know, get the girl all upset and everything."

"Make her jealous?"

"More than just that," Heather says. "Chicks get jealous if their boyfriends just look at some-body else. But some guys, they like to start these cat fights."

"I just can't relate to that. When I was a teenag-er, girls never came to blows."

"They do now. Believe me."

"So what happened with Kimberly?"

"One night the guy comes knocking on her window, and she climbed out thinking they were going on a date like they had been. But Lindsay was hid in the guy's pickup. She had this baseball bat."

"And attacked Kimberly with it?"

Heather seems excited. "Beat the living shit out of her. Broke her jaw, knocked out a bunch of teeth. Kim had to have plastic surgery."

"And what happened to Lindsay over the incident?"

"She got probation, had to leave school. You know Adrianne testified in court, at Lindsay's probation hearing? Lindsay hated Adrianne's guts over that."

"I'd heard as much. Didn't Lindsay become a suspect after Adrianne died?"

Heather nods. "The cops questioned her and had her take a lie detector. Look, I got to get back." She starts to rise.

"One more thing," the interviewer says. "If Adrianne knew about this, wouldn't she have been more cautious?"

She seems oddly thoughtful. "You might think so. But, hey, Kimmy getting beat up, that was just one thing. Adrianne wasn't messing with Lindsay's boyfriend or anything."

"No, I mean, the overall picture. Wouldn't it make her think twice about sneaking out, staying out all night?"

"Why would it?" Heather says. "Just because something like that happened to Kimmy, who'd think it would happen to them?"

Adrianne got off from work around dark and bummed a ride with one of the Golden Fried Chicken's delivery cars. She got home, a modest brick house, around seven in the evening. It was in a neighborhood of small one-stories a mile or so down the road from the Golden Fried Chicken. Waist-high fences separate backyards containing swing sets where children play. Adrianne wasn't born in Mansfield, but since she'd lived in the house ever since she was five, anywhere else was the faintest of memories to her.

It's easy to point fingers after something tragic happens to a child, accusing her parents of neglect. Media accounts of abused, battered, or murdered kids bring up images of beer-swilling fathers and swinging mothers. In Adrianne Jones's case, nothing could be further from the truth.

Roy Jones is an excellent mechanic, but his income is modest. Had he stayed in Dallas, conditions would have worsened as his neighborhood crumbled around him, so in 1984 he brought his family to Mansfield. He commuted to work, battling freeway traffic on the hour-long trip, so that his three offspring—Adrianne was the eldest, along with two younger brothers—could grow up in a pleasant rural environment away from the dangers of the city.

Like her bearded, no-nonsense husband, Linda Jones is a worker, every nickel of their dual incomes needed to support their family. Her salary and tips come from giving massages to Mansfield's gated community dwellers in a beauty parlor, and fifty- and sixty-hour work weeks are not unusual for her. She spends every spare moment at home, tidying up, tending her yard, riding herd on her kids. A lively teenager is a handful under any circumstances, and given their struggle to make ends meet, was even more of a problem for Linda and Roy.

If anything, the Joneses were overly strict with Adrianne. They did not let her out of the house on school nights, did not allow her to date until her sixteenth birthday. They relaxed her nine o'clock weekend curfew just months before her death, and then ordered her home no later than ten. They had no inkling, of course, as to the extent of Adrianne's after-midnight wanderings; only a week before, Roy had caught her crawling in the window around dawn and had reacted by nailing her windows down.

Linda spent the afternoon and early evening of December 3 painting her kitchen. Though she was tired to the bone, when the Joneses' family dogs—two German shepherds and a collie, one of the shepherds, named Thor, being Adrianne's personal pet—set up a ruckus announcing her daughter's arrival, Linda perked up. She climbed down off her stepladder and cleaned off the paint. It had been awhile since Linda had spent any time with Adrianne and, given their respective schedules, this quiet Sundey evening would be the last chance she'd have for quite a while to come.

By the time Linda reached her daughter's doorway, Adrianne had stripped out of her Golden Fried Chicken uniform. The room had a waterbed, Pearl Jam and Annie Lennox posters covering the walls, a Mickey Mouse phone, a ten-dollar used stereo with tapes scattered about on the dresser. Adrianne pulled on blue and green flannel workout shorts, put on a gray T-shirt, then a long-sleeve knit with REGION I CROSS-COUNTRY REGIONALS 1995 lettered across its front. She turned to her mother and said, "Can we go for a workout, Mom?"

Linda sagged against the jamb wearily. "I've been painting all day, girl."

Adrianne flashed the grin that could move mountains. "It'll pick you up, then. Come on, Mom. Can we?"

Linda didn't want to, but knew she'd give in. The membership in the Huguley Fitness Center was a luxury the Joneses really couldn't afford, but did for Adrianne's sake. Family rules dictated that Adrianne couldn't leave the house after dark unchaperoned. Adrianne had a driver's license but no wheels as yet—the 1940s-model pickup in the driveway was a restoration project that Roy had planned in order to give Adrianne transportation—so Linda had two choices. She could refuse her daughter's request altogether or go with her. And it had never been in Linda to say no to her eldest child.

"Yeah, all right," she finally said. "Just give me a minute to put something on."

So Linda Jones went in her bedroom for her own gym clothes, not really wanting to make the half-hour drive to and from the fitness center. If it would please her little girl, however, Linda was willing to go the extra mile. In the months to come, Linda would be very glad that she went along.

The Huguley Fitness Center, a modern facility with Nautilus machines, full-body workout units, and electric stairclimbers, is in Crowley, sixteen miles to the west of Mansfield. Like all rural small towns just down the road from one another, the communities interact; Mansfield people do business in Crowley and vice-versa, and the residents of the towns all know each other, just as they know the residents of Midlothian, Cedar Hill, and Burleson, all dots on the map within a twenty-mile radius of Mansfield. Kids from neighboring towns all hang out together—other than on certain fall Friday nights when their football teams have a go at it.

Linda and Adrianne had an hour-long workout, Linda going through the motions, Adrianne getting after it with a teenager's boundless energy. Though Linda's fanny was dragging a bit, the exercise picked up her spirits, and her daughter's amazing physical condition gave her a sense of pride. Adrianne went through a series of sit-ups, leg raises, presses and curls, did thirty minutes on the stair climber, and hardly seemed to break a sweat. They relaxed a few minutes with fruit drinks at the bar and made the drive home around ten p.m.

On the next-to-last ride of Adrianne Jones's life, she was in an oddly pensive mood. "What do they call a person who tells you why you act the way you do, Mom?" she asked.

"I'm not sure what you mean. Like, a psychiatrist?"

"No, that's a doctor. More like, someone who does counseling."

"Well," Linda said, "there's a behavioral analyst. They get a rundown on the way you behave, then tell you why it is you act like that, and if there's something wrong with the way you're acting, they can straighten you out."

Adrianne settled back in the seat. "That's what I want to be, then."

"A behavioral analyst?" Linda said.

"Yep." Adrianne hugged herself. "After college, Mom. That's just what I want to be."

Adrianne got a call shortly after returning home, and lied to her mother about it. Unfortunately for the murder investigation, the true identities of the callers wouldn't come out for quite some time.

The phone rang at a quarter until eleven. Calls after ten were not allowed in the Jones household, and with Linda narrowing her eyes, Adrianne snatched up the portable receiver as teenagers are wont to do. "Hello?" she said breathlessly, then turned her back and began a hushed conversation.

Linda was having none of it. She walked firmly around and faced Adrianne, eye to eye. "Who the hell is that?" she said.

Adrianne palmed the receiver. "It's David," she said.

Linda Jones didn't know David from Adam's ox. "David who?"

Adrianne looked cross. "David from cross-country. He's *really upset*, Mom," she said, and then showed Linda her back once more, talking in a near whisper. She carried the phone down the hall to the laundry room to dump tomorrow's school clothes in the washer.

In fact, Adrianne's caller wasn't "David from cross-country" at all; it was Tracy Smith, the nineteen-year-old bodybuilder with whom she'd sneaked out of the house on the night her father caught her. Tracy was off limits both because of the sneaking-out incident and because Linda and Roy thought he was too old for her. In the days immediately following the murder, police were to discover that Tracy was the caller and assume that "David from cross-country" was a made-up name. They were dead wrong. "David from cross-country" was someone very much on Adrianne's mind.

With Linda badgering her to hang up, Adrianne continued on the phone long enough to muddle the police investigation even further. The Jones telephone is equipped with call waiting, and as Adrianne talked to Tracy, another caller beeped through. She clicked off the line for a second, then came back on to tell Tracy that the intruder was still another boy, a seventeen-year-old dropout from Mansfield High named James Drummond. He had called Adrianne earlier at the Golden Fried Chicken to arrange for her to sneak out with him after her parents went to bed.

The conversation didn't last more than three or four minutes. Linda stood firm and, threatened with having her mother seize the phone and cut her off, Adrianne gave in and terminated the call.

Linda Jones was livid. "That's enough, young lady. You get your butt in bed."

Adrianne showed a look of disgust, walked into her room, and flopped onto her waterbed. As Linda watched through the partly open door, Adrianne put on earphones, turned on the stereo, and folded her arms across her chest. She noticed her mother and, as a final act of defiance, turned off the light in her room.

Linda Jones went to her own bedroom and climbed wearily into bed beside Roy, who was already snoring. With the younger kids asleep and Adrianne listening to the stereo, the house went dark around eleven-fifteen.

It didn't remain dark for very long. Forty-five minutes later, certain that her parents were dead to the world, Adrianne switched her bed lamp on. Sitting at her vanity, she put on diamond stud earrings and a gold necklace from which a pendant in the shape of the letter A dangled. It was midnight, the witching hour, time for the fun to begin.

# 3

As Adrianne Jones prepared for midnight, another teenage girl was already on the prowl. She took Interstate 20 and then Highway 287 south into Mansfield, having left her home in Fort Worth shortly after Adrianne and Linda departed the Crowley fitness center. She used her right hand to drive, while her left hand rested woodenly in her lap. The hand was still hurt like the blazes, three of her fingers having been nearly severed just a couple of months earlier.

Though not plain, Diane Zamora would never stand out in a crowd. She was as near to Adrianne Jones's opposite as was possible. Whereas Adrianne was outgoing and fun-loving, Diane was quiet, reserved, and little difficult to get to know. While Adrianne tended to dress in attention-getting outfits, Diane's tastes ran to loose-fitting dresses, modest pants, severe blouses, dark colors. Her glistening blue-black hair was cut short and close around her head, her eyes deep brown, her Hispanic ancestry having blessed her with lovely copper-colored skin and high, prominent cheekbones.

Even her speech was different from Adrianne's. Adrianne talked in a Jessie May Clampett twang, Diane in a quiet, cultured tone. Other than the slightest Hispanic rolling of her r's and the pronunciation of "sh" words with a "ch" sound, Diane's English is perfect. As well it should be, since English was one of her top subjects at Crowley High. Her Spanish is another story; Diane speaks the Spanish of the Texas streets, a curious mixture of Spanish and English words— "I quit" becomes *"mi quito"* and a bath, not the beach, is *"una playa."* Though Diane can recite hundreds of Bible verses in Spanish, she doesn't write a word of her grandfather's native language, having learned Spanish as a baby at home but having written only English since she started school.

She made the turn on Highway 287 and drove into Mansfield to the block where her boyfriend lived.

David Graham didn't have the same problem in getting out of the house that most of the teenagers did. He merely dressed in camouflage fatigues, laced up his combat boots, and strode out of his room without worrying about the noise he was making. His father was older than most adolescents' parents—sixty-one, in fact—had retired from his school principal's position a number of years ago, and always turned in early. David's mother, a teacher twenty years younger than his dad, had separated from his father two years ago and lived across town. Since she had been the one who'd kept the most watchful of eyes on her son, David now did pretty much as he pleased. This night he paused to hoist a canvas tote bag and walked outside to wait at the curb. Though the day had been warm, the nighttime temperature had slid down into the fifties.

The tote bag he was carrying contained his father's loaded 9mm pistol, two twenty-five-pound barbell weights, and a fifth of bourbon.

Not only did David have more freedom than most of the other kids, he looked older as well. He was a strapping six-footer with dark brown hair cut in a half-inch burr, his bearing military, and could easily pass for a man in his mid-twenties. Though he wasn't to graduate from high school for six more months, he had already decided on an Air Force career and looked the part.

Headlights stabbed the darkness as a small Mazda hatchback came around the corner. David picked up the bag and marched firmly toward the auto. The back door opened and the interior lights flashed on, illuminating Diane's features as she sat behind the wheel. In spite of her grim expression, David thought she was the most beautiful girl he'd ever seen.

James Drummond didn't have the slightest idea that Adrianne had already fingered him as a murder suspect. That night he didn't have much of an idea about anything, in fact; he was later to tell police that he was too drunk to remember where he'd gone or what he'd done.

At least that's the police detectives' story. Once Adrianne's murder became a national event, he was to claim that he wasn't drunk at all. According to James Drummond, his mind was numb with antidepressant drugs, and considering the lawsuit in the wings, it isn't surprising that his story differs widely from the police department's version. Whether the cause was alcohol or prescription medicine doesn't really matter at this point; James's lapse of memory was to cause him serious problems.

It's pretty well established that James Gregory Drummond left his parents' home in his midnight blue Isuzu pickup truck around eleven, about fifteen minutes after Linda Jones had forcefully terminated Adrianne's telephone call. It wasn't unusual for James to be out late. The husky seventeen-year-old with a shock of dark brown hair wasn't a student; he'd had serious mood problems for several years, had taken prescription drugs for his condition since the age of fourteen, and had dropped out of Mansfield High while still a sophomore. During the past year he'd held several jobs, none for very long, and had less than a sterling work record. As a dropout moving from job to job, and with a penchant for memory lapses, James would fit the suspect's mold to a T.

Exactly where James wandered that night no one really knows. He might've bought some beer, and he might've merely driven around. Adrianne's friends say that he had a crush on her, and he very likely did. The two had gotten to know each other when working at nearby jobs in downtown Mansfield the previous year, and ever since then James had called Adrianne just about every day. His phone number was in Adrianne's address book, and he was one of the boys with whom she went riding late at night on a fairly regular basis. And Adrianne had told one of her Golden Fried Chicken coworkers that she was meeting James later that night. If he did have a crush on her, it was apparently a one-way street; the consensus of opinion among the pretty blonde's friends is that Adrianne "was tooling poor old James Drummond around."

James made a stop on that fateful night that turned out very badly for him. Sometime around two a.m. he pulled his pickup to the curb in front of Adrianne Jones's house. No one knows if he got out of the truck, and James says he doesn't remember. Actually, he says he doesn't remember being at the Jones home at all; his answer to police questioning was, "I might have been there. I just don't know." What happened inside the house at two o'clock, however, leaves little doubt that James was on the premises.

At exactly two, Adrianne's younger brother heard her alarm go off. This wasn't an unusual occurrence, for Adrianne often set her alarm go off and then took a nap before going off on late-night forays. But on this occasion no one was there to turn off the buzzer, and finally her little brother got up to investigate. Adrianne wasn't in her room. After the child shut off the alarm, he watched through the window as a dark-colored pickup sped away from the curb in front. Her brother didn't wake his parents to tattle on his sister. He assumed that Adrianne was off for some late-night partying once more, and went back to bed.

Odds are strong that James did in fact approach the house—Adrianne's window was near the front—only to find that Adrianne had stood him up and was already gone. When the alarm went off, James most likely panicked, leaped in his truck, and squealed away into the night. In months to come, he would very much wish he'd hung around to offer explanations.

Adrianne wasn't there when James arrived because she'd left a few minutes before one in the morning, shortly after a knock on her bedroom window. Since she couldn't raise the window because it was nailed shut, she communicated with the person outside using a series of hand signals. She motioned for quiet, fearful that her late-night visitor would wake the dogs, then pointed to show the visitor he should wait out front for her. Adrianne snuck past her sleeping parents' door and out through the living room. She left the door unlocked. She wanted to be certain that once the fun was over, she'd be able to get back in.

Over in Burleson, another small town near Mansfield, seventeen-year-old Bart Horne, Jr., B.C. to his friends, lay on the floor in his sleeping bag. B.C. was a military kind of guy, and sleeping on the floor was as much a part of his regimen as jogging through his neighborhood in full battle gear and backpack. His stiffly starched uniforms—Civil Air Patrol and Crowley ROTC—hung in his closet. B.C. plans a career as a Marine, and will no doubt make a good one.

B.C. was awakened around three in the morning when a heavy fist pounded on his window. He put on his silver wire-framed glasses and peered outside into the darkness. It was David, his number one running buddy and mentor in the Civil Air Patrol. B.C. raised the window and said hello.

Something was wrong. David cowered against the window, his breathing ragged, his eyes wide in distress, his normally strong tenor voice halting as he said, "Let us in. You've got to let us in."

Us? B.C. squinted. He hadn't noticed the small figure crouched alongside David before, and now looked in question at his friend.

"Diane's with me," David hissed. "Come on, let us in."

B.C. hesitated. Creeping out of the house had never been much of a problem, but admitting a twosome in the middle of the night with his parents sleeping in the very next room was something else again. And Diane . . . well, B.C. didn't exactly *dislike* Diane. It was just that since she'd come along, David hadn't been quite the same. B.C. preferred things between him and David the way they used to be. Finally he nodded, unlatched and removed the screen from his window. "Quiet, now," he whispered. "If my old man catches us, it's my ass."

David boosted the petite girl up, and B.C. helped her over the sill. She'd barely touched down on the floor before B.C. regretted his decision to let the pair inside. Diane immediately huddled in the corner, crying softly, repeating over and over, "It hurts. Oh, it hurts, it hurts." As B.C. turned back to the window, David was already coming in through the opening.

David Graham and B.C. Horne look very similar. Both are a shade over six feet tall with military burr haircuts—though B.C.'s is blond while David's hair is brown—and both stand ramrod straight like drill corps cadets. Indeed, the military is the main thing they have in common; David is a year older and was the ROTC commander at Mansfield High, and B.C. was to have the same honor at Burleson High during his senior year. They had met at Civil Air Patrol meetings held at Spinks Airport on Rendon-Crowley Road between Crowley and Mansfield. David was to become one of the most decorated cadets in Civil Air Patrol history, and B.C. was proud to serve as his underling. The two buddied around a lot in the pre-dawn hours, going to ice cream parlors, drinking beer, or just driving like hellions down dusty roads, but this time something was different. David had never brought anyone to B.C.'s house before, not in the three years they'd known each other, and the fact that his companion was Diane Zamora made the whole thing even spookier. David and Diane, when together, normally kept to themselves.

Diane continued to moan in the corner, and B.C. was getting nervous.

David's features were stern. "You're my best friend, B.C. My best damn friend."

B.C. couldn't argue with that. "Yeah, I guess I am," he said.

"For starters," David went on, "this never happened. Us being here. You never saw us tonight, okay?"

B.C. was later to tell police that he didn't have any idea what kind of trouble the teen lovers had gotten into, and didn't want to know. More than anything, he wanted them to leave. He felt an odd fear as David continued to stare coldly at him. Finally B.C. said, "Sure, if you say so." Then he tried a little humor. "As far as I'm concerned, you're invisible."

David never cracked a smile. "Good. Now, we need to use your bathroom."

B.C. indicated the door. "Sure, yeah, you know where it is. Just remember, my old man . . ."

"No sweat, buddy," David said, started to turn, then fixed B.C. with a stare. "Just remember you haven't seen us." Then he helped Diane into the bathroom and closed the door.

B.C. trembled as he sat on the bed and listened to the shower hiss through the closed door. What was going on? He didn't want to turn on the light for fear of waking his parents, so he plugged in a tiny electric Christmas tree on his desk.

After what seemed like hours, the shower stopped running. Seconds later, David came through the door in his underwear. He held out a hand, palm up. "I need a pair of shorts."

B.C. rummaged in his drawer and came up with some old athletic shorts that David quickly

put on. "My best friend," David said again, then
went back into the bathroom.

A few more minutes passed, after which both
David and Diane came out, David carrying his
boots and fatigues in a bundle under his arm.
Diane was no longer crying; she was dressed in
the same jeans and pullover as when she'd
climbed in through the window, and her hair was
sopping wet. David said to B.C., "Give us a
minute, will you?" Then, without waiting for an
answer, David and Diane lay down on top of B.C.
Horne's sleeping bag while B.C. sat in silence on
his bed. David and Diane wrapped their arms
around each other as Diane repeated over and
over, "I'm cold. I'm cold, David. God, I'm so
cold."

Finally the lovers rose and walked arm in arm
back to the window, where David paused and
turned. "You didn't see us, B.C.," he said.

And B.C. repeated, as though reciting from
memory, "I've never seen you. Right, I never
have."

David nodded, helped Diane climb outside,
then hoisted his leg over the sill, his fatigues
pressed against his bare chest and his boots dan-
gling from his fingers. "You're my best friend,
B.C.," he said. "*Semper fi.*" With that, David
Graham went out the window, and the lovers disappeared in the darkness.

B.C. went over and replaced the screen, wondering for a time whether the crazy incident had really happened at all. Had he been dreaming? No matter. He'd told David that he'd forget what he'd seen, and that's just what he would do. After all, he thought, friends in combat are only as good as their word.

# 4

The Serendippity Hair, Nail, and Massage Salon didn't open until ten o'clock, and Linda Jones did massages by appointment and didn't have anything on her calendar until Monday afternoon. So she slept in until seven-thirty, long after Roy had left for his job. Groggy from staying up past her usual bedtime, Linda made her way outside to get the paper. The incredible weather had held; a bright sun shone over a bank of fluffy clouds, and the thermometer was to hit the seventies for the third consecutive day. It seemed more like spring than the middle of the Christmas season.

Linda took the paper inside and laid it on the breakfast table, then carried a few soiled things back to the laundry room for placement in the washer. When she raised the lid, she realized something was wrong.

Her thoughts flashed back to the previous night, when she'd chastised Adrianne as the teenager rattled on over the phone. Yes, Linda was certain. During the call Adrianne had carried the portable telephone to the washer as she'd dumped some school clothes in. The clothes, still wet, were now clinging to the sides of the washer tub as they'd been ever since completion of the spin cycle, which would have been shortly before midnight. Like most teenagers Adrianne wasn't particularly organized, and she waited every night until the last minute to wash whatever she was wearing to school the next day. Classes would begin in less than a half hour, and there was no way to dry the outfit in time. What would Adrianne wear? More important, why hadn't she gotten up as yet? Curious, but with no sense of dread, Linda walked into Adrianne's room.

What she found there sent a tremor up her spine. The bed hadn't been slept in; there was a depression in the spread where Adrianne had laid in a huff, listening to her stereo last night, but she'd never thrown back the covers. Further, Adrianne's running shoes, the only shoes she ever wore, were side by side on the floor.

Linda hurried into the kitchen, her stomach doing flip-flops. Maybe her daughter had decided to run to school and had left early. But barefoot? No way.

Linda sat rigidly at the breakfast table until eight o'clock, then called the high school and asked if Adrianne had arrived for class that morning. The first-period rolls hadn't been turned in as yet, so the telephone secretary asked if Linda could wait while the office dispatched a runner to the classroom. Yes, Linda would hold. She sat and listened for what seemed an eternity, until the assistant principal clicked on the line. The runner had gone to the classroom, and the teacher had double-checked her attendance record. As of that moment, Adrianne Jones had yet to arrive.

Her heart pounding, Linda then called the police station. According to Mansfield detectives' records, the missing-persons report came in via phone at 8:09 A.M., but an official investigation couldn't begin until Linda filled out some paperwork. In order to facilitate completion of the form, the dispatcher sent a squad car to the Jones residence. The uniforms dutifully recorded their time of arrival in their log book, and knocked on Linda's door at 8:23.

What Linda Jones didn't know was that her daughter had already been found. Gary Foster out by Joe Pool Lake had found her. Only she was dead, with her skull caved in and two bullet holes marring a pretty young face that would never smile again.

The call Gary Foster made that harrowing morning was not to the Mansfield police, however. By a quirk of political maneuvering when the lake was made, the place where her body was found lies within the boundaries of Grand Prairie, Mansfield's larger neighbor to the north.

When viewed in an aerial photo, Joe Pool Lake resembles a man from the waist down, with the dam on the northern end of the valley forming his belt and his legs angled off in a southwesterly direction. The city of Grand Prairie occupies a large area beyond the north rim of the dam, and Mansfield is opposite our strange-legged creature's right big toe. The two cities appear to be across the lake from each other.

But this isn't entirely true. While Mansfield and Grand Prairie had similar modest beginnings during the latter portion of the nineteenth century, Grand Prairie's location on a direct east-west line between Dallas and Fort Worth gave it greater accessibility to the two metropolises, and when bedroom commuter communities sprang up during the sixties and seventies, Grand Prairie's population far outstripped that of its southwesterly neighbor. By the time the lake reached the drawing board stage, Grand Prairie had a tax and voting base sufficient to pull a few strings in order to expand its boundaries. The end result was that Joe Pool Lake now lies almost entirely in Grand Prairie's city limits, and a thin finger of Grand Prairie extends all the way to the Mansfield city limit sign. If Gary Foster's property was a couple of hundred yards to the west he'd be in Mansfield; as it is, his 911 call went to the Grand Prairie police department. In light of subsequent events, Grand Prairie would just as soon they hadn't taken the case.

Because of the remoteness of the crime scene, the emergency unit didn't arrive until a good half hour after the call went in. Once there, the uniformed police verified that indeed a body lay on Gary Foster's land, secured the area with yellow tape, called for the crime-scene unit, medical examiners, and detective crews. Finally they stood guard around the perimeter of the protected area, averting their gazes from the grisly sight beyond the fence. Every policeman who viewed the remains alongside Seeton Road made the same observation: The murder of Adrianne Jones was as brutal as any in memory.

Grand Prairie police headquarters is in close proximity to a string of auto graveyards along Highway 80 east of town. To reach the headquarters from Dallas, one drives west on Jefferson Boulevard past twisted wreckage piled as high as office buildings. In decades past the area was known as "Fence City, USA," and the nickname had nothing to do with the tall wire barriers surrounding the junk dealers' places of business. Car thieves far and wide used to haul their booty to East Grand Prairie for the quickest available under-the-table sale. The salvage business has legitimized itself in recent years, but the neighborhood has lost none of its atmosphere.

Grand Prairie suffered the same growing pains in the late sixties as did Mansfield in the eighties and nineties, and in 1973 its undermanned police force relocated from one-horse, center-of-town facilities to its present space. Today the city of 150,000 employs 172 cops and, big-town style, breaks its detective force into categories designated under the Texas Criminal Code: Crimes Against Property (burglary, theft, and fraud) and Crimes Against Persons (including assault and homicide). Its crime-scene units and police labs employ the latest in technology, and its officers attend college classes and FBI training sessions. Chief Harry Crum dresses in suit and tie and belongs to the Kiwanis and Rotary clubs. On a smaller scale, Grand Prairie law enforcement operates on a level with that of any major city.

The Crimes Against Persons detective team that drew the assignment on Seeton Road consisted of a pair of veterans, Dennis Clay and Dennis Meyer. Case assignments are on a strictly random basis; the call comes in, and the shift lieutenant sends out whichever team happens to be on duty at the moment. Once a case belongs to a particular pair of detectives, it's theirs until the file is closed by arrest, conviction, or a determination that further pursuit is a waste of time. Homicide files remain open in perpetuity, though at times the trail grows cold enough that they are placed to the rear of a file drawer and virtually forgotten. Through no particular right of seniority or superior investigative skills to his partner's, Detective Clay became the team's lead man. Clay and Meyer drove their unmarked city vehicle over winding backroads, skirted Joe Pool Lake to its southwest shoreline, and arrived in front of the mailboxes on Seeton Road a half hour after the crime-scene and emergency medical units.

One look at the corpse had made the medics' job relatively simple. They had a representative from the coroner's office pronounce the victim dead on the scene, took the body's temperature for estimation of the time of death, then stood aside until the crime-scene unit finished gathering evidence. The medics waited patiently; the CSU procedure was going to take awhile. As Clay and Meyer approached the barbed-wire fence, white-coated lab techs sprayed, vacuumed, inspected the ground nearby, and snapped pictures of the body.

Crime-scene photos are among the most effective of prosecutorial tools, but even the hardened police crew working the scene kept their faces averted as they moved around the body. They knew immediately what forensics evidence would later bear out. The mutilated condition of the body, coupled with the fact that Adrianne was fully clothed, left little doubt that this was no sexual crime, and odds were strong that whoever killed Adrianne had done so in a rage. But how could anyone harbor such hatred for a pretty sixteen-year-old girl?

So much blood had soaked into the ground and stained the grass around the body that, from a distance, Adrianne appeared to be lying on a bright red blanket. Two medics gently moved the corpse while a third dug shovelfuls of earth from around her head and stored the blood-soaked dirt in an evidence bag. Then they removed her clothing, being careful not to disturb any fibers clinging to her shorts, T-shirt, and pullover, and preserved the garments as evidence as well. Detective Meyer noted on his report form that the corpse wore one diamond stud earring in her pierced right earlobe, and correctly assumed that the other earring had been lost in a struggle. Adrianne's gold necklace was missing as well, but the necklace's absence wouldn't be discovered until much later. Her legs were badly scratched, presumably from crawling through the barbed-wire fence as she'd tried to escape the murderers. The fluttering piece of cloth that had originally attracted Gary Foster's attention matched a rip in Adrianne's shorts. Three of her fingernails were torn; medics carefully encased her hands and her head in plastic wrappers.

Meanwhile, there wasn't much for detectives Clay and Meyer to do. Standard operating procedure in crime-scene investigation is for the detective team to canvass the neighborhood, conducting interviews to determine whether anyone has seen or heard anything, but the nearest house to Gary Foster's place was nearly a mile away. Investigators would later make perfunctory inquiries of the neighbors, all to no avail. Not even the still-trembling Foster was to be of much help. He had been home the night before, but neither he nor his wife had heard a thing. At one point the detectives heard the beep of a metal detector, and then took possession of two 9mm shell casings that a crime-scene tech had found a few feet from the body. The shell casings were to be the only evidence of any real value recovered from the murder scene.

Finally, once the corpse's clothing was bagged as evidence and its head and hands preserved in plastic, the crime-scene people waved in the medics. They put the remains in a body bag and carried the body to their ambulance for transportation to the Tarrant County Morgue. As the ambulance headed down Seeton Road, the detectives transmitted Adrianne's description to Grand Prairie's main police headquarters. For several hours to come, the body found in Gary Foster's field was to remain unidentified.

Meanwhile, in Mansfield, Steve Noonkester studied a missing-persons report, dated and signed by a frantic Linda Jones, stating that Adrianne had vanished sometime after eleven-thirty on Sunday night. It was nearing noon on Monday, so Adrianne had been missing for twelve full hours. Using a list provided by Linda Jones, Noonkester had questioned some of Adrianne's classmates, the Golden Chicken's manager, Tina Dollar, and had taken a survey along the route that Adrianne normally took to school. No one had seen her, but several people had a number of things to say about Adrianne. Given the pretty teenager's penchant for late-night wanderings, Noonkester assumed he was looking for a runaway, but the fact that Adrianne hadn't returned home by now made the police-man very nervous. If missing kids don't turn up in a few hours, usually coming home when the first hunger pangs hit them, they seldom turn up at all. Experience told Noonkester that if he didn't find Adrianne very soon, his department had a problem on its hands.

Steve Noonkester is a large man, nearly six and a half feet tall and weighing nearly three hundred pounds. With a thick gray mustache to match his hair, he's a twenty-seven-year veteran. In 1989 he forsook the big-city wars for a more laid-back job with the city of Mansfield as deputy chief, and toward the end of 1996 he was to take over as act-ing chief when the head man resigned. In smaller law enforcement outposts such as Mansfield, deputy chiefs take on a variety of tasks in addition to their administrative duties; on December 4, Noonkester was the day-watch head of the Criminal Investigation Division.

Many of the police officers in Mansfield and its neighboring towns are veterans of inner-city strife who have served out their pension-vesting time. The smaller cities can use the experience, and the veteran officers can use the simpler lifestyle. Until recent years Mansfield law enforcement duties consisted of rousting an occasional drunk or lying in wait behind highway billboards for unsuspecting speeders passing through. As big-town problems have filtered into Mansfield, however, a policeman's duties have changed a great deal.

Noonkester reviewed the missing-persons report once again and realized that he had less than nothing to go on. The object of his search was a white female, sixteen years of age, five feet four, weighing a hundred and thirty pounds with blond hair and green eyes, a description that could fit any number of teenagers. Sometime after midnight she'd left her home, either alone or in the company of others, and no one had seen her since. Procedure dictates that descriptions do not go out over the national network until someone has been missing for twenty-four hours, so other than checking inquiries from nearby jurisdictions, there was little for Noonkester to do. He absently scanned requests for information coming over the computer. Grand Prairie's query about the body on Seeton Road had yet to reach the system.

Adrianne's unexplained absence didn't cause concern at the Mansfield High attendance office because of recent changes in state scholastic laws. Prior to the 1994–95 school year, Texas school districts were required to categorize absences as either "excused" or "unexcused," depending on whether the student had written permission from home, but after decades of learning that many notes from mother or dad are forgeries, and random policing of irresponsible parents—many of whom used the excuse system to duck laws requiring them to keep their kids in school until they are sixteen—the legislature took a different approach. Today a student exceeding nine absences per semester isn't promoted to the next grade. The result is that school officials don't patrol the absentee list with the same vigilance as before. On the morning of December 4, Adrianne was one of several dozen who weren't at school.

Though within a day Adrianne's murder would be on everyone's lips, on that Monday morning the administration was more concerned over a different student's absence. The school's highly regarded ROTC unit was up for inspection, and the cadets had come to school with spit-shined shoes and polished brass. ROTC met during second period, the nine o'clock session, and halfway through the period the principal's office received a call for help. The cadets couldn't proceed because there was no one present to give the inspection. Among the missing that day was the ROTC batallion commander, a by-the-numbers cadet named David Christopher Graham. No one connected Graham's absence to that of Adrianne Jones. And for many months to come, no one would.

Jerry Graham was worried that his youngest son, David, had stayed out all night again, but was fairly certain that no harm had come to the boy. His three older kids had never caused much grief in the Graham household—two had graduated from college and a third was in pre-law—but ever since Jerry's separation from Janice, his wife of twenty years, David had been pretty much out of control. Now that he was eighteen, he was considered an adult, so Jerry Graham had stopped trying to dictate David's comings and goings, and kept his fingers crossed in the hope that things would work out in the long run.

Jerry Graham is a wiry man with the square-jawed look of someone accustomed to standing his ground. He has the ruddy complexion of a man often exposed to the weather, and since his retirement finds various methods of keeping himself busy during the day. On December 4 he got up early, noted that David wasn't in his room, went out and got the paper, and set about fidgeting, waiting for his son to come home. He knew better than to call the police. David was an adult, not subject to any teen curfews, and without evidence of foul play the cops wouldn't look for the boy.

The Graham home, like that of Roy and Linda Jones, is located in the older section of Mansfield. It's a modest one-story, though not as modest as the Jones house, on a block of well-kept yards. He's lived there since David was a baby.

Janice Graham, Jerry's estranged wife, didn't work until David was a teenager, so the boy's early upbringing didn't lack for maternal affection—or discipline. The Grahams are Southern Baptist, and Janice is as devout as they come. Even before David could read and write, he could hum the tune to "That Old Rugged Cross" or "Bringing in the Sheaves," and even knew most of the words. Attendance at Sunday services—both morning and evening for Baptists—and Wednesday night prayer meetings was a given in the Graham household, and twice a year, spring and fall, revivals turned churchgoing into a seven-day proposition. Additionally there was vacation Bible school for two weeks in the summertime, midweek visits to the sick and afflicted, and home Bible study in between.

David never questioned mandatory church attendance until he was halfway through middle school, the age at which peer pressure set in. He was bigger than nearly all of his classmates, and in Texas larger boys almost always try out for the football team. David was no exception. He reported for tryouts every fall beginning with his sixth-grade year, even though he wasn't very good. His physical coordination never caught up with his size, and even today David is a bit awkward. Plus, he didn't have the necessary killer instinct needed for football. The result was that David spent most of his football career on the bench and finally dropped out altogether in his sophomore year.

Yet David's participation in the sport brought him a new circle of friends. Always before his playmates had been kids he'd met in Sunday school, most with similar upbringings. In athletics, however, David met boys who had never even been to church. David began to question: *If he doesn't have to go to church, why do I?* As David grew older, he continued to attend services by parental decree, but his constant dozing brought frequent sharp elbow nudges from his mother.

Oversized and clumsy, David was also painfully shy. He was terrified of girls, and never dated at all until his senior year. He was bright—his IQ is exceptional, in fact, and he achieved A's and B's in honor classes. But his intelligence caused him to be terribly aware of his own shortcomings. His lack of aggressiveness in football made him the butt of many jokes on the part of his teammates, a situation which multiplied his lack of self-confidence tenfold. As David moved agonizingly through teenhood, both Jerry and Janice Graham realized that their son desperately needed involvement in something—anything—in which he could excel.

David Graham says that he decided on a military career at the age of nine, when his father took him to an air show at Fort Worth's Carswell Air Force Base. His first recorded encounter with any branch of the armed services came during his freshman year at Mansfield High when, at his parents' urging, he enrolled in ROTC.

It is sad but true that there are two organizations at most large high schools in America, the band and the ROTC, which create close friendships among their members but, alas, bring derision from fellow students as well. Kids who are, for reasons known only to God and their contemporaries, considered cool around campus sneeringly refer to members of the band and ROTC as "band weenies" or "rotsy queers." Peer pressure causes many who would otherwise benefit from these organizations to drop out early in high school; to carry on requires a stiff upper lip and a hide as thick as a turtle shell. Those who go forward in spite of everything usually reap enormous benefits. In David Graham's case, he would go on to be accepted by the Air Force Academy. Yet it also bred a rigidity that would have disastrous consequences.

### Close-up

The young man, wearing a plaid button-down shirt and stylish wire-framed glasses, carefully considers his answer. "I guess David was in, well, kind of a different zone," he finally says.

"Took things more seriously?" the interviewer asks.

"He wasn't serious about everything. But when it came to ROTC, hey, the guy was something else."

"Lived and breathed it?"

"A lot of us felt that way. Doing good in ROTC was important to me, too, but I had other things going. I mean, he was rotsy commandant, like, big deal, most of us thought, great. But David acted like they'd just appointed him General Schwarzkopf or something."

The young man's name is Steven Cooper, and he's just completed his first semester at Texas A & M.

"He was the take-charge type?" the interviewer says.

"More than just that. You're talking a guy that wore combat boots to school every day. Even when it was hot and we all wore shorts, there he was with those freaking boots on. David didn't care if he looked like a dork or not."

The interviewer ponders his next question. "If you were to sum it up, how was he different from, say, the other guys in ROTC?"

"Well, everybody liked it or they wouldn't have been in it, right? And a lot of them, I didn't, but a lot of them joined the Civil Air Patrol so they could play soldier more than once a week. You'd pass David in the hall, even on days we weren't wearing uniforms, he was just as apt to salute you as he was to say hi. And those drills, on rotsy day, if you didn't march just right, he might walk up behind you and jab your butt hard, then get right up in your face like he was the drill instructor."

"He was into all things military, then. Did you ever meet Diane Zamora?"

Cooper shakes his head. "No, I told you I was never in Civil Air Patrol, and she went to a different high school. But everybody knew he had a chick over in Crowley. One time he made us an announcement that he was engaged, and said they'd get married after he graduated from the Air Force Academy. But I never saw her in person, didn't even know her name until all this was in the paper."

"How about Adrianne Jones? You know her?"

This brings a nod. "Sure. She was kind of ditzy, but I mean, this was a good-looking girl."

"Well, did you ever see her and David together?" the interviewer asks.

Cooper's eyes widen. "No. No way. Adrianne was into a different kind of guy, maybe a few of the freakers. But the idea that a girl like her and a guy like him, the idea they'd even get together at all . . . that's even weirder than that murder and everything."

Jerry Graham heard his son come in around mid-morning, when the back door slammed and heavy footfalls marked David's passage through the kitchen into his bedroom. There was the sound of movement inside David's room for a few minutes, followed by silence. The elder Graham walked quietly to David's door and peeked in. David was under the covers and appeared to be asleep.

Jerry Graham went back in to read the paper, relieved that his son had come home unharmed. He would never ask David where he'd been all night; experience had taught him that David would answer any question with silence and a surly stare. Missing a day of school wouldn't hurt David scholastically. His grades were good, and the results of his SAT's placed him in the top ten percent of all the college applicants in America. None other than Vice-President Al Gore had recommended David for appointment to the Air Force Academy the next fall, and the boy was a cinch to get in.

David's constant late-night roaming, though, was definitely something to worry about. His obsession with the girl from the south end of Fort Worth, Diane Zamora, was a point of concern as well. Diane was the only steady girlfriend David had ever had, and Jerry Graham thought his son should try playing the field. David, Jerry thought, should finish college and have his career goals lined up before he became serious over any female.

But overall, David's future continued to look bright, and a year in the strict environment of a military academy should set his behavior straight. In the meantime, Jerry Graham kept his fingers crossed, and hoped against hope that David's late-night prowling wouldn't get the boy into serious trouble of some kind.

Grand Prairie's request for information on the body found on Seeton Road flashed on the computer screen around three in the afternoon, and Steve Noonkester read the data with a feeling of despair. The description of the corpse fit Adrianne Jones perfectly. Still, Noonkester couldn't sound any alarms until he was sure. Carrying Adrianne's picture in his briefcase, the Mansfield policeman set out for the Tarrant County Morgue.

Tarrant County law enforcement—including the sheriff, the district attorney and the medical examiner's unit—serves thirty-five police departments from its Fort Worth headquarters, and dissects its murdered corpses in one of the more dismal parts of town. Oldtimers call the section the Hospital District because Fort Worth's oldest medical institutions—All Saints', St. Joseph's, and John Peter Smith—are nearby. John Peter Smith is the county hospital, and as such is the main receiving facility for Fort Worth's gunshot victims.

Steve Noonkester pulled into the lot behind the morgue at four in the afternoon. Fifteen minutes later, after comparing the photo with the mutilated face on the autopsy table, he was on his way back to Mansfield. No longer just a copy with a missing-persons report on his desk, Noonkester was now the bearer of tragic news.

Mansfield High School's attendance office dutifully loaded its computer at the close of classes, and the computer's auto-dialer phoned the following message to the Jones residence around five in the afternoon: "Your child was absent today from one or more classes today at Mansfield High. If you have questions regarding your student's absence, please call the assistant principal's office in the morning." The Joneses' answering machine took the message, which came about the same time that Steve Noonkester, head bowed, told Roy and Linda in their living room that their daughter had been brutally murdered.

# 5

Fictional television and movies aside, the person you least expect seldom commits murder in real life. If the victim's husband or wife had the best motive, coupled with any possible opportunity, that's whom the cops normally arrest. Policemen never herd the suspects into the drawing room and, Hercule Poirot fashion, elicit a confession through a hypothetical question-and-answer session. Veteran detectives also know that if they don't identify the perpetrator within twenty-four hours after discovery of the crime, more often than not the killing remains unsolved. In the case of Adrianne Jones, the cops were hot on a suspect's trail in less than a day.

Crime-scene evidence is among the most misunderstood of all police procedure. While hair and fiber samples are of the utmost importance in convicting the suspect once he or she is identified, seldom does anything found at the scene of the crime lead police to persons unknown. Only after legwork and logic leads to apprehension does crime scene evidence nail the suspect down.

Other than the 9mm shell casings recovered from the scene, forensics evidence gave detectives Meyer and Clay little to go on. The chunks of bloody earth shoveled carefully into evidence bags showed only Adrianne's DNA; the one diamond earring torn from Adrianne's lobe and the gold necklace ripped from around her neck were items that the police were never to find. Her coarse flannel clothing should have yielded loads of clinging trace evidence, but, remarkably, all hair or cotton fiber vacuumed from Adrianne's shorts and pullover came from inside Roy and Linda Jones's home. It was a given that the killer or killers had taken Adrianne to the murder scene in a vehicle of some kind, and police could only hope that if they ever found the truck or car, fiber from Adrianne's clothes would be recovered inside.

The autopsy on the body wasn't of much use, either, other than to show that Adrianne had struggled fiercely before she died. Her left index finger was badly broken and stuck out at an odd angle. Bruises and abrasions covered her chest and neck. The fierce scratches on her legs, police assumed, came from the barbed-wire fence, and they further assumed that whoever had killed Adrianne caused the scratches when they dumped her body into the clearing. The M.E.'s office easily concluded that they were dealing with a homicide (no matter how obvious it seems that police have discovered a murder, the death isn't officially a homicide until the medical examiner so rules), but determining the cause of death was a problem. The crushed skull and the two bullet holes were all fatal wounds. Since all three injuries had been inflicted about the same time, the M.E. didn't know if Adrianne had been first bludgeoned and then shot, or if the killer had shot her to death and then attacked the body in an act of rage. Whichever wound had caused her death, this wasn't a sexual crime; the body was fully clothed, the undergarments undisturbed, and there was neither presence of semen nor the vaginal or anal bruising that invariably accompanies a rape. Detectives Clay and Meyer kept copies of the crime-scene unit's and medical examiner's reports for future reference, then set about compiling a list of Adrianne's enemies.

The list turned out to be a very short one. Clay went to the Jones home on the morning of Tuesday, December 5, and searched Adrianne's room, even as Roy and Linda made their daughter's final arrangements. The detective moved quickly but quietly; a shroud of grief hung over the house, and Clay didn't want to upset the family any further. He forced the grisly image of the corpse out of his mind, and zeroed in on Adrianne's room and its contents.

The surroundings were typical for a sixteen-year-old: Adrianne's Mickey Mouse telephone was on the floor in easy arm's reach from her waterbed, and an Annie Proux tape was inserted in the stereo slot. "No More I Love You's" was Adrianne's favorite song.

Clay examined the closet and found the usual teenage clutter—gum and candy wrappers, ballpoint pens, notebook paper covered with notes from classmates, mostly wadded and tossed, all strewn among a jumble of dirty clothes on the floor—along with a sparse wardrobe: three pairs of jeans, T-shirts showing Dallas Cowboy emblems, Pearl Jam and Stone Temple Pilot photos, a few simple blouses, a long blue dress with a pale pink flower pattern, a pair of loafers whose soles were barely worn, more evidence that Adrianne either went barefoot or wore running shoes ninety percent of the time. Clay backed out of the closet and looked around. Most teenagers keep their innermost secrets tucked low in bureau drawers, and the detective went over and had a look.

In the top drawer of her dresser, buried under a pile of bras and Jockey-for-Her cotton briefs, Clay found a soft-covered address book with alphabet tabs. There were entries on almost every page, mostly first names followed only by telephone numbers, and a few out-of-town entries that included mailing addresses. It was a start, if nothing else. Carrying the address book, walking softly, Detective Clay left the house and silently closed the door.

Running down the people listed in Adrianne's address book was slow going. She seemed to have ignored the alphabet tabs and written down first names in no particular order. Many of the numbers had changed or were disconnected. Worst of all, everyone with whom Meyer and Clay did make contact had no useful information and furnished ironclad alibis. The detectives drew a total blank until they came to the C's, where there was a name listed only as "Kimberly" followed by a phone number. Meyer made the call. A pleasant woman answered, saying, "Horton residence."

"Detective Meyer," Meyer said professionally, "Grand Prairie police. Is Kimberly there?"

There were several beats of silence, after which the woman said, "I'm Kim's mother. May I help you?"

Meyer hunched over his desk. "We're investigating the death of Adrianne Jones, Mrs. Horton. Did you know her?"

"Yes."

"Well, your daughter's number was in Adrianne's address book ma'am. We're checking to see if anyone knows someone who might have wanted to hurt her."

There was more silence over the line, accompanied by shallow breathing. Finally Kim Horton's mother said, "Lindsay Wade. She beat Kim nearly to death, Detective. If I were you, Lindsay Wade is the first person I'd be contacting."

The lead regarding Lindsay Wade turned out to have little effect on the overall scheme of things, but in retrospect, Lindsay Wade probably did furnish an unintentional insight to Adrianne's real killers. Lindsay was a frail sixteen-year-old at the time of the murder, and two years earlier had very nearly killed someone herself. Her victim was a close friend of Adrianne's named Kimberly Horton.

Kimberly is today a wispy thin teenager with green braces on her teeth, was a track and cross-country teammate of Adrianne Jones, and after Adrianne's death stayed zonked on cocaine most of her waking hours for half a year. At the age of fourteen she had begun a sexual affair with Lindsay Wade's boyfriend, who was seventeen at the time. The affair mostly took place in the wee hours when so many Mansfield teens had a tendency to roam. Kim steadfastly claims that the boyfriend had told her he and Lindsay were through.

A few months into the affair, Kim heard a knock on her window around one in the morning. She peered outside; the boy stood in the moonlight, beckoning. Kim quickly climbed into shorts and a T-shirt, raised the window, and climbed outside. Hand in hand she went with the boy to his pickup. The boy went to the driver's side, leaving Kim at the passenger door. As she prepared to climb in, the door slammed open, knocking Kim off balance. Something hard crashed into her head; dazed, she fell to the ground.

An enraged Lindsay Wade charged from the truck, wielding a baseball bat. Kim screamed and tried to cover her head with her arms. Lindsay raised the bat and brought it smashing down.

Kim's features tightened a bit as she remembers. "I can't tell in words how much it hurt. She was absolutely beating the shit out of me, and I was on the ground and couldn't move. There was so much blood in my eyes I couldn't see a thing, and that goddamn bat just kept hitting me over and over. I'm pretty sure I passed out for a few seconds, because when I woke up Lindsay wasn't hitting me anymore. I laid there and kept my eyes shut until that pickup started and drove away, and I believe they thought I was dead or Lindsay would have beat the shit out of me some more. Finally, I was able to crawl up on our porch and ring the doorbell and wake my mom." She becomes very serious. "Lindsay was going to kill me, mister. I know that as well as I know I'm sitting here talking to you."

Kim's injuries bear out her fear that Lindsay

had murder on her mind. Emergency room personnel first determined that Kim had a fractured cheekbone, a broken nose, and a concussion, and then delayed treatment of those wounds until they had used forty-five stitches to close the lacerations on the back of her head. Kim's parents filed an assault complaint with Mansfield police, who immediately arrested Lindsay Wade and, unable to charge her as an adult, held her in juvenile detention. Through her lawyer, Lindsay reached a plea-bargain agreement with prosecutors and pled guilty to the charges in return for a probated sentence. Among the witnesses against her at her sentencing hearing was Kimberly Horton's good friend Adrianne Jones. She repeated the same story in court that she'd earlier told Mansfield High officials: Lindsay had made no secret of the fact that she wanted Kimberly dead. At the time of her sentencing, Lindsay Wade was fourteen.

The incident was the subject of Mansfield gossip for many months, discussed by adaults and teens alike. As their parents shook their heads in disbelief and horror, one group of Mansfield adolescents traded guarded nods. In their eyes, Lindsay had done nothing but defend what was hers, and as a violator of the code, Kimberly Horton had received her just reward.

David Graham knew about the beating, of course, though just how much influence Lindsay

Wade had on his later actions is purely speculation. Certainly if he wanted to think about it one way, it set a precedent.

Roy and Linda Jones had their daughter's remains cremated. Three days after Gary Foster had found Adrianne's body on his land, the Joneses held a small private service at Mansfield's United Methodist Church. Roy Jones, his voice quaking with emotion, eulogized his daughter as the finest child a man could ever hope for. At the close of the service, at Linda's request, Annie Proux's "No More I Love You's" played in the church as the family broke down in tears.

People have their own ways of dealing with tragedy. While Roy Jones has for the most part grieved in silence since Adrianne's death, Linda Jones has become a regular speaker at meetings of victims' and public interest groups. She wants Adrianne to be remembered, and does everything possible to achieve this goal. In the months following the murder, long before the case became an international media event, Linda gave speeches at Victims' Outreach, the Mansfield Chamber of Commerce, and the Fort Worth Stop the Violence Peace March and Youth Rally. As her daughter's ashes reside inside her home, Linda wants to be heard.

A week to the day after the memorial service,

Linda went to Mansfield High School for a second ceremony, this one held near the track where Adrianne so loved to run. The cross-country, track, and soccer teams along with the Fellowship of Christian Athletes and members of the high school staff gathered solemnly to watch a tree planting in Adrianne's honor. Afterward, countless teenagers hugged Linda, cried uncontrollably, and assured Linda that they had loved Adrianne. Among those offering condolences, tears streaming down his face, was the tall blond six-footer who ran on the cross-country team and bossed the school's ROTC unit, a sad, reserved young man named David Christopher Graham.

Early on in the case, detectives Meyer and Clay took a hard look at Lindsay Wade. On probation for beating Kimberly Horton, Lindsay had dropped out of school and worked a series of fast-food jobs, and no matter where the detectives turned for information, they were hearing Lindsay's name. Not only did Kimberly's mother suggest that Lindsay, now sixteen years old, might be Adrianne's killer, one Mansfield High School student after another pointed the finger in Lindsay's direction as well. According to the kids—the ones who would talk, at any rate—Lindsay had hated Adrianne because of her testimony in the probation hearing, and given Lindsay's history of violence, picturing her as a murderer didn't require much stretch of the imagination.

Suspicion aside, however, there was no physical evidence to link Lindsay to the crime. The detectives had her in for questioning twice; on both occasions the teenager brought her parents and her lawyer along and refused to give much more than her name. It's standard for defense lawyers tell their clients, when under investigation, not to say a word to the cops, but policemen tend to interpret a person's refusal to talk as evidence of guilt. Meyer and Clay tried fighting fire with fire. They got the necessary court orders requiring Lindsay to give her fingerprints and blood specimens—presumably more to upset the girl and her lawyer than for any other reason; at that point the police had zilch in the way of crime-scene evidence with which to compare Lindsay's samples—grilled Lindsay's coworkers and friends incessantly in an attempt to determine her whereabouts on the night of the murder, and leaked information to the press that she was their number one suspect. Nonetheless, in the fact of all the heat the detectives could muster, Lindsay kept mum. Her lawyer told her to dig in for the long haul, because it looked as if she had quite a mess of trouble in store.

She certainly would have had, if Detective Meyer hadn't received a call that would lead to a more cooperative suspect, James Drummond. As things turned out, he rescued Lindsay from the frying pan and put his own feet into the fire.

The call Meyer received was from Tracy Smith, the bodybuilder who had called Adrianne on the night of the murder. Tracy Smith is nineteen years old and lives on his own in a trailer house over in Venus, near Mansfield on the Midlothian side, and Linda Jones was probably correct in thinking he was too old for her daughter. Tracy, who spends a lot of time in the gym, met Adrianne through the Golden Chicken's drive-through window. It was Tracy who'd sneaked Adrianne out of the house on the night that Roy caught her coming in and subsequently nailed her windows down. Thick and muscular Tracy may be; dense between the ears he is not. The moment he heard about the murder, he decided to contact the police before they came looking for him.

In truth, Tracy would have been a serious suspect if he hadn't had an ironclad alibi. He had been out of town with his parents on the night of the murder, and detectives already knew that his call to Adrianne had been via long distance. What he told Detective Meyer spun the investigation off in a completely different direction. When Meyer learned that James Drummond had beeped through during the call, the policeman paid immediate heed. Waiters, busboys, and cooks at Golden Fried Chicken had already told the cops that during her last day on the job,

Adrianne had indicated that she was meeting James later on that night. Further, James's name and number were listed in Adrianne's address book. Meyer and Clay learned that James was a high school dropout with a less than pristine work record, and decided immediately to have James come in. When he arrived at the station minus lawyer or parents, the detectives gave him the standard hey-old-buddy, thanks-for-coming-in-and-clearing-this-up greeting, hauled the unsuspecting youngster into a back room, and firmly drew a bead on him. What follows is a dramatized account of James Drummond's version of his meeting with Clay and Meyer. Under advice of the attorneys defending the detectives—along with the city of Grand Prairie—in James Drummond's lawsuit, the detectives have yet to comment on the matter other than to acknowledge that the meeting indeed occurred.

The interrogation room at Grand Prairie police headquarters is at the rear of the Crimes Against Persons section, with a window facing the auto graveyards. James sat with his back to one wall, made nervous by the two detectives staring at him. Clay played the good guy, Meyer the bad, which, considering the detectives' appearance, is about the roles one would expect. Dennis Clay is a mild-mannered man of average height, with neat dark hair and a trimmed mustache. Dennis

Meyer stands six foot plus and has a thick, broad-shouldered body. Both are patrol-car veterans who have seen duty in some of the nastier parts of town. Clay's manner was casual and businesslike, while Meyer regarded the suspect with just a hint of a scowl.

"Hi, James," Clay said. "Thanks for coming in."

"Sure, yeah." James did his best to sound self-assured.

Clay showed a bland smile. "Coffee? Coke or something?"

James cleared his throat. "Glass of water, please."

"Sure thing," Clay said. "Dennis, could you ... ?"

Meyer took his cue, went over and opened the door, and called for one of the office people to bring some water. He returned to his seat and fixed James Drummond with a stare.

"Like I told you over the phone, I'm Detective Clay and this is Detective Meyer," Clay said. "We want to talk to you about some things we've been hearing."

"You mean, about me?"

"Well, yeah, about you and some other things. This shouldn't take long, but we hear a rumor, we got to clear it up."

There was a moment of silence as James continued to fidget and the detectives continued to stare.

Clay said, "First of all I'll ask, have you got any idea what it might be we're hearing?"

"I got hassled for drinking a couple of times," James said. "But not lately. I don't do that anymore."

"You don't?"

"Well, maybe a beer every once in a while, but nothing serious. I'm taking this medicine."

Clay blinked. "You think this is about underage drinking, James?"

James licked his lips and shifted nervously in his chair. "I don't do any drugs."

"Nice to know," Clay said. "But this isn't the narcotics bureau. That's down the hall."

A sharp knock interrupted. Meyer got up and took a glass of water in through the door, and set the drink in front of James as Clay forged ahead.

"So we're not talking drinking and we're not talking dope," Clay said. "You do a lot of running around at night, James?"

"Well, some. Go to movies . . ."

"Hey, what we're talking about, there aren't any movies showing that late. I'm talking, two or three in the morning."

"Sometimes I might," James said. "If I got things bothering me."

"What would be bothering you? A young guy like you, you should be happy-go-lucky."

James rested his forearms on the table and

clasped his hands, "You know, things. Like my job, maybe."

"What else?"

"I don't know."

"What about girls?" Clay said.

"They might bother me, if I knew any." James laughed, a high-pitched, squeaky sound.

"You don't know any girls? Hey, if I was running around late at night, I'd sure want a lady with me." Clay looked to Meyer. "Wouldn't you want a girl, Dennis, if you were running around at night?"

Meyer's gaze never left the suspect. "Yep," he said. "But maybe James here, he likes to be alone."

"Well, say, James," Clay said, bending forward, "how about last Sunday? Were you out then?"

James's chin lifted a fraction. "Last week?"

"Yeah, last week. The night of the third of December, morning of the fourth. You out running around?"

"Could have been. I do most nights."

Clay stroked his chin. "Most nights. This Sunday in particular, you have anything to drink?"

James averted his gaze. "I might've."

"Yeah? Where all did you go?"

"I don't really remember. Just driving around."

Clay expelled a long breath and looked at Meyer. Meyer folded his arms and didn't say anything. Finally Clay said, "What do you think, Detective Meyer?"

Meyer showed the suspect a hard look. "Hmm?" he said to Clay.

Clay slowly lowered his eyelids to half-mast. "I don't think James here knows what this is all about."

"Oh, I think he does," Meyer said.

"He don't act like he does," Clay said. "You got anything you want to ask this boy?"

Meyer pushed his hair back. "Yep."

"Okay, Detective Meyer," Clay said, gesturing toward James. "You got the floor."

"Tell you what, James," Meyer said, "you know Adrianne Jones?"

James snuffled through his nose. At this point, with the murder fresh in the papers, everyone in Mansfield had either known Adrianne personally or at least knew who she was. Nonetheless, James tried weakly, "Who?"

"Adrianne Jones, James," Meyer said. "Come on."

"I don't," James said, then seemed to swallow a lump the size of a grapefruit before saying, "I don't believe I do."

"Come on again," Meyer said. "I mean, we're just talking here. You tell me you don't know Adrianne Jones, I'm going to wonder if you're leveling with us."

"Now, look." James spread his hands, palms out. "I didn't have anything to do with that."

Clay broke in, looking incredulous. "Have anything to do with what, James?"

"With that . . . you know."

Meyer's features set like stone. "I don't know nothing about any *you-know*. We just asked you if you were acquainted with Adrianne Jones."

"Well . . ." James was trembling, gasping for breath. "She's dead."

Meyer continued to bear down. "Who's dead? This girl you don't know?"

Practically in tears now, James pleaded, "Look, I think I should leave."

"You don't want to leave yet, we're just getting started. Now, did you know Adrianne Jones, or didn't you?"

James bowed his head. "Yeah, so I knew her."

"Then why would you tell us you didn't? Sounds a little funny to me, James."

"Because . . ." James stopped, then practically screamed, "Because you guys are scaring the shit out of me."

"You oughtn't to be scared, seeing as how you didn't have anything to do with it. Why you scared, James?"

James didn't answer and kept his head lowered. His shoulders began to shake, and he emitted a soft sob. The detectives exchanged a look. Clay nodded to Meyer, who went on.

"James, we don't want to hassle you unnecessarily. Let me ask you, did you go by Adrianne's last Sunday night?"

James looked off in the distance. "I don't know."

"How the hell can you not know?" Meyer said. "Don't you know where you were?"

"I'm not sure," James said.

"You're not sure." Clay leaned back and scratched his head. "You must have been awfully drunk, you don't even know where you were."

"I told you, I take this prescription."

"Mmm-hmm. Let's try something else. You ever been to the place where they found her body?"

"I don't even know where it is."

"You mean, you don't read the paper?"

"Never, sir. Never read it. I only heard that Adrianne was dead."

Meyer produced a crude cross, made from two sticks held together with red wire. "How about this, James? You ever seen it before?"

James watched the cross wide-eyed. "What is it?"

"It was hanging on the barbed-wire fence out where they found the body," Meyer said. "We thought maybe the asshole that killed her put it there. Which isn't you, right?" (Actually, as police were later to learn, a friend of Adrianne's named

Jeff Lackey had fashioned the cross and hung it on the fence as a memorial.)

James squirmed. "Never saw it before. I told you, I don't even know where they found her."

Clay continued to look thoughtful. "Okay, James, I'm going to ask you a hypothetical. You know what a hypothetical is?"

James stared as if in shock.

"Okay," Clay said, "a hypothetical, that's a bullshit question. It's where I ask you about some fictional event, and you answer just like the fictional event really happened. You ready?"

James's eyes welled with tears. "I'll be glad to try."

"Say you'd killed somebody," Clay said, "which you say you didn't, but imagine you did. Where would you put the body?"

"Where would I . . . ?"

"Yeah, around Mansfield, which is where you live. Where would you dump the body, James?"

"How would I know? I don't think I want to talk to you anymore."

"Just a hypothetical, okay?" Clay said. "You're driving around with this body, where would you put it? Just answer that one thing for me, then you can go."

"Just a hypothetical?" James hugged himself.

"Just imagining, yeah," Clay said.

"Oh, I don't know," James said. "I guess, out by the lake someplace?"

"One of those lonely roads out there?"

James stood up. "Somewhere like that. Listen, can I go now?"

Meyer and Clay exchanged a look. "You know, that's odd," Clay said. "Because that's just where they left her." He grinned. "Looks like you hit the nail on the head, James. Yeah, we're finished here. But do us a favor and don't get out of pocket, okay?"

When examined with the benefit of hindsight, James Drummond's answers to the detectives' questions during that initial session make perfect sense. Just like Tracy Smith, James feared that because of his relationship with Adrianne, he could become a suspect in her murder. He was on pins and needles before he ever came to the station in response to the detectives' call, and his denial that he even knew Adrianne was nothing more than a knee-jerk reaction to the detectives' confrontational attitude. In securing their later warrant for James's arrest, Meyer and Clay stated that he'd pretty well described the murder scene in answer to a hypothetical question, and in truth he had. However, it's also likely that any Mansfield resident would have supplied the same answer. The twisting roads around Joe Pool Lake are the only isolated body-dumping spots in the area.

Nonetheless, after their first contact with James

Drummond, the Grand Prairie police seemed to rule out Lindsay Wade and all other suspects, and concentrate on building a case against him alone. It's a possibility that zeroing in on James Drummond might have caused detectives to overlook avenues which could have brought the investigation to an earlier close.

Among the facts dismissed by police was the statement from Linda Jones that Adrianne had identified her caller on the night of the murder as "David from cross-country." During the initial stage of the investigation, Detective Clay did go to the high school and interview members of the track and cross-country teams in the coach's office. All of the athletes were cooperative, but none offered information that could help in finding the killer. One of those speaking to the detective was David Graham. Clay asked if David knew of anyone who might want to harm Adrianne.

"I can't think of anybody," David said. "To tell you the truth, other than from running, I just didn't know her that well."

"You don't know who she was dating?"

"I didn't know she dated at all. She was only a sophomore. A lot of those girls, their parents won't let them yet."

"David," Clay said, "did you by any chance call Adrianne on the night of December third, at her home?"

David's head tilted in curiosity. "Why do you ask?"

"Because her mother told us she had a call from 'David from cross-country.' Could that be you?"

David smiled helpfully. "Well, I'm the only David on the team, but it couldn't be me. I've got a girl. We're engaged. If I were to start calling someone else and Diane found out about it, well, she just might kill me, sir."

# 6

If not for the shadow hanging over its principal players, the story of David Graham and Diane Zamora would read like a formula movie romance. Boy meets girl. At first they can't stand each other, but as time goes by, they overcome their differences and fall in love. Like Romeo and Juliet, they cling to each other despite the slings and arrows hurled by family and friends. Boy fouls up and almost loses girl. Boy spares no end to redeem himself. Girl forgives him, and the lovers stroll hand in hand into the sunset. A camera-ready plot, if David's redemption hadn't come about through an act of unspeakable violence.

Like David, Diane says that she decided on a military career when she was very young. Her family—parents, aunts, uncles, and cousins—concurs, recalling that when Diane was about twelve, she came home and announced that she wanted to be an astronaut. It's a noble aspiration for a youngster to want to travel in space, of course, but Diane's experiences in uniform indicate that she was never cut out to be a soldier to begin with. It's more likely that her application to the U.S. Naval Academy was prompted by her desire to escape from a childhood of near poverty.

Newspaper, television, and magazine accounts of the Graham-Zamora-Adrianne Jones tragedy have pictured both Diane and David as honor students, popular both at school and around the community, the brightest of stars in their neighboring rural towns. And it's true that Mansfield and Crowley, only sixteen miles apart, once had a lot in common. But the birth of Joe Pool Lake, which created the population surge in and around Mansfield, had no effect on Crowley's growth, and Crowley today is still little more than a dot on the map. As for Diane Zamora, well, she's never lived in Crowley, and if not for certain quirks in the laying out of Texas school districts, her name never would have been associated with Crowley at all.

Crowley, population 7,900 is a stone's throw east of Interstate 35, about fifteen miles south of the Fort Worth city limits. That's fifteen miles today, though thirty years ago the distance was double that figure; as Fort Worth has grown, so have its boundaries. State school district funding in Texas is based on enrollment, and during the latter half of the twentieth century the migration to cities from rural areas caused many small districts to shrink to the point that they couldn't pay the bills. As rural schools closed one after the other, districts were forced to consolidate in order to provide education, the result being that kids in farming communities today often ride buses for twenty miles or more in order to attend classes. Such was the case with Crowley, which, along with several neighboring towns, consolidated during the seventies into the Crowley Independent School District. Today, however, Fort Worth has expanded to the point that much of the southern portion of the city is within the Crowley ISD, and many big-town kids are in the unique position of having to travel to the country in order to go to school. With the influx from the heavily populated areas of South Fort Worth, Crowley High today has an enrollment of two thousand, a quarter of the population of the town itself. Most of Fort Worth included in the Crowley ISD is upper-middle-class, but there are fingers of Crowley ISD boundaries that include neighborhoods of near-ghetto living conditions. Diane Zamora is from one of those neighborhoods.

### Close-up

"I was like everybody else," the husky teenager says, "when all that came out in the papers. I looked her up in the annual. I think I remember her, but I'm not really sure. They came and went."

"Kids from other areas?" the interviewer says.

He nods. "Sure. They came to class and all hung out to themselves, and when school was out, we wouldn't see them again until the next day. We didn't run around with any of them."

The boy's name is Greg Bishop, and he graduated from Crowley High in Diane Zamora's class; he's taking classes at Tarrant County Junior College.

"But when Diane won the appointment to the Naval Academy, didn't that make her better known?"

Greg shakes his head. "I knew several kids applying to those service schools, but not her, not really. They probably announced where she was going during our baccalaureate service, but there were hundreds of kids getting this scholarship and that scholarship, and you can't remember them all." He grins. "I even got one, five hundred dollars from the Lions' Club, and you see where I'm going to school."

"So you'd say, Diane wasn't all that popular."

He shrugs. "What's popular? I guess I was popular, with my own friends, and she probably was with hers. But those South Fort Worth kids going to school in Crowley?" He ruefully shakes his head. "I wish I could help you more. But the truth is, we didn't really know any of those kids."

* * *

The area of small wooden houses and streets of cracking asphalt is largely Hispanic, many of its older residents having been born in Mexico. While the immigrants adhere to the culture of their ancestors, their offspring sometimes thumb their noses at the old ways, so it's not unusual to hear conversations where parents rebuke their children in Spanish while the kids sass back in English. Early mornings are filled with comings and goings, as men and women in work clothes, suits, or business dresses head for their jobs, passing scruffy men with bandanas tied around their heads as they slink home after a night on the streets. In December there are traditional Christmas trees hung with ornaments, but also there are giggling blindfolded children in the yards, whacking at piñatas hung from trees with Louisville Slugger baseball bats. As is to be expected, the residents of the area are Catholic for the most part, and in many living rooms there are statuettes of *El Cristo* on the cross.

Diane Zamora is third generation. Her father, Carlos (shortened to Carl, just as many Mexican-Americans Texanize their Hispanic given names), grew up a few miles to the north. He's an athletic, strikingly handsome man with a neatly trimmed black beard. He wooed and married Gloria Mendoza twenty years ago, and Diane is the eldest of four. Gloria works in obstetrics at

All-Saints Hospital, and Carlos is a licensed electrician, but these are only their weekday jobs. So much does Gloria's father influence the Zamora family that Miguel Mendoza's calling bears ample mention here.

El Templo de Juan Tres, Diez y Seis (The Temple of John 3:16—"For God so loved the world," the verse begins) occupies a white graffiti-decorated building near the South Freeway. Every Friday night and Sunday morning the sanctuary fills to capacity with men who seem a bit awkward in suit and tie, women whose starched dresses are the only showcase garments in a threadbare wardrobe, and children whose faces are scrubbed for perhaps the only time during the week. El Templo de Juan isn't affiliated with any secular denomination; acceptance of Jesus as *El Hijo de Dios* (the Son of God) is the only requirement for membership. Miguel Mendoza is pastor, youth director, treasurer, and custodian, and performs whatever additional duties that are necessary to the Work. He pays the church obligations out of congregational donations—which sometimes, particularly after first-and-fifteenth paydays, are considerable—and lives on the remainder.

As in any depressed area, religion is a powerful guiding force in South Fort Worth. Where there is a language barrier, church is even more important to the underprivileged. Fort Worth, a modest-sized city, lists twelve congregations with all-Spanish services in its southwest section, with titles such as Templo Centro Cristiano, Templo del Buen Samaritano, and there's even a Templo Emanuel for Mexican-Americans of the Hebrew faith. As is the case with Miguel Mendoza at El Templo de Juan, these churches are one-man shows.

Sunday services at El Templo de Juan 3:16 begin with a rousing session of hymns in Spanish, backed by a robed choir and a five-piece band. A communion of grape juice and unleavened bread follows the singing, and volunteers take up the weekly offering in chrome collection plates. When Miguel Mendoza finally approaches the podium for his sermon, a hush falls over the audience. He's a powerful, mesmerizing speaker, his intense fire-and-brimstone delivery often continuing for an hour or more, punctuated by occasional shouts of *"Bueno, padre"* from the congregation, the Spanish equivalent of cries heard so often in Southern fundamentalist churches.

Carlos Zamora is a major participant in the musical portion of his father-in-law's services, playing the saxophone with the band, joining in with the choir whenever he lays his instrument aside. Gloria Mendoza also sings in the choir, as a soprano. Until a little less than a year ago, her daughter Diane sang by her side.

Like David Graham's upbringing in the Baptist

faith, Diane Zamora's strictly supervised early years revolved around the teachings of her grandfather. Attendance at El Templo was a weekly event never questioned by Diane or her younger siblings. Before Diane was old enough to participate in services, the Zamora children sat in one of the auditorium's most prominent rows. After church were family gatherings, cars lining the street in front of Miguel Mendoza's home, just a few blocks from El Templo. It was a major event in Diane's life when, at the age of twelve, she was permitted to join the choir.

Ties in the Hispanic family unit are strong. Uncles, aunts, and cousins are more like immediate family than they are distant relatives, and the Zamora-Mendoza clan is outspokenly proud of Diane even today. Most of her kin blame David for the mess in which Diane finds herself; in the Graham family, of course, the feelings are just the opposite.

Even as a ten-year-old, Diane was considered responsible, and was the first choice around her neighborhood for baby-sitting. During the media blitz surrounding Adrianne Jones's murder, reporters have often contacted members of the family in search of quotes. When questioned about the crime, Zamora relatives immediately change the subject to talk about how smart she is, and what a wonderful young woman she had become until David led her astray.

Diane was a good student as well, and she could be found reading all the time. Everywhere she went—on baby-sitting assignments, on the school bus, or even to and from church services—Diane took her books along, and her grades reflected her efforts. Unlike David Graham, she isn't intellectually gifted; her SAT scores fall somewhere in the mid-level range. But through work and determination she always made her grades. Diane's high school marks were in the upper ten percent of her class.

Media reports of Diane's popularity at Crowley High are terribly exaggerated. The fact is that she was an outsider in Crowley, being bused to school from South Fort Worth, and fellow students barely recall Diane if they remember her at all. The principal of the high school told the *Fort Worth Star-Telegram*, shortly after Diane's arrest that until the announcement of her appointment to the Naval Academy, he'd never even met the girl. Diane is shapely and well coordinated, and during her sophomore year tried out successfully for the drill team, but the cost of several show-time outfits, not to mention traveling expenses to and from performance sites were more than her family could bear, and she had to drop out. She was also a member of the National Honor Society. At David Graham's urging she tried out for the cross-country team during her senior year, but according to team members, she hated running and never was much of a factor on the squad. In sum, Diane went through Crowley High in virtual anonymity.

Like most parents, Carlos and Gloria Zamora wanted nice things for themselves and their children, but often bit off more than they could chew. Lacking the cash to buy clothes for their kids and furnishings for their home, the Zamoras fell victim to credit-card debts, and during the eighties filed for personal bankrupcty on three separate occasions. Carlos, though a licensed electrician, had difficulty in finding and keeping work. Once the power company shut off the Zamoras' electricity, and Diane studied by candlelight for three weeks until her parents could scrape up the money. It's to the Zamoras' credit that they never begged; pride is as much a part of the Hispanic culture as are religion and family. Though Miguel Mendoza would have certainly helped them, Carlos and Gloria got by on their own as best as they could. They had a number of family cars, a series of junkers from used lots on Ft. Worth's seedy East Lancaster Avenue. As long as Carlos made his fifty-dollars-a-week payments on time, he had transportation, but several times he was late and found himself on rubber heels instead of rubber wheels.

Given her financial background and outsider status at Crowley High, Diane couldn't help but struggle with feelings of inferiority. She went quietly to school, head down, paid attention in class, and immersed herself in her assignments. She seldom dated, if at all. Daughters in Mexican-American families are subject to the strictest of upbringings—even today arranged marriages in the Hispanic community are not unusual. So, her studies her only real interest and her social life revolving around people she met at El Templo de Juan, Diane moved timidly toward adulthood. It's likely she would have grown up and married a nice boy from the neighborhood had not Carlos Zamora begun an affair when Diane was around fourteen.

The woman's name is Connie Guel. She doesn't place blame for the affair, other than to say that she'd just been through a divorce and was vulnerable at the time. For months after Diane's arrest she kept a low profile. Then, once his daughter's predicament had made Carlos Zamora somewhat of a media figure, she submitted to an interview with the *Ft. Worth Star-Telegram* that amounted to an exposé on Carlos's private life.

A surprising number of affairs begin in church under just such circumstances: a recently divorced woman seeks comfort in religion, then succumbs to advances from a church member or pastor to whom she has turned for guidance. In Connie's case, she went to church, handsome

Carlos was there as saxophonist and member of the choir, and he and Connie had an affair that lasted several years.

Regardless of who started the affair, both Connie and Carlos must shoulder equal blame for the lack of discretion in disguising their relationship. They appeared in public together numerous times, both in supermarkets and noontime restaurants, and there is no environment where tongues will wag more quickly than in the Hispanic community. Diane heard rumors that her father was running around within a month after the affair began, but refused to believe the stories until near the end of her sophomore year. One afternoon while Gloria was at work and Carlos was out of a job, he took his mistress home and into his bedroom.

In the midst of the lovers' afternoon of passion, Diane unexpectedly came home from school. There followed a scene in which Carlos sat numb in the living room while his daughter cried and screamed hysterically, and while Connie Guel cowered alone under the covers. During the confrontation between father and daughter, Connie dressed and crawled out the window. Neither Carlos nor Diane ever told Gloria about the incident; she was left to learn of it when the affair was broadcast in the morning paper for all to read.

Diane, of course, was crushed. All is high drama in the teenage world, and the fact that her father—her mentor both in life and in the teachings at El Templo de Juan—had been unfaithful to her mother was more than Diane could bear. Outwardly she didn't change a great deal, and continued her devotion to her school work. But just as David Graham began to doubt after joining the football team, once Diane's image of her father was shattered, her religious faith began to wane.

Diane understood that her only real chance to escape her humble background lay in going to college, but also knew that the odds were strongly against family help in the paying of tuition. Her high school counselor, sympathetic to her situation and impressed by Diane's grades and work ethic, suggested that she apply to one or more of the service academies. Not only was room and board in these institutions free to the student, the academies paid enrollees a service person's salary as well. A degree from a service institution practically guaranteed a successful career as an officer. Additionally, as a double minority—a Hispanic female—Diane would receive priority consideration on her admissions application.

Diane needed no further encouragement. Not only did she find out everything she could about

West Point along with the Air Force and Naval academies, she also learned from the Air Force recruiter that nine congressional academic appointments a year were reserved for top cadets from the Civil Air Patrol. The CAP, a volunteer Air Force search-and-rescue unit, had a squadron stationed at Spinks Airport, a tiny field on the road from Crowley to Mansfield. Brimming with excitement, Diane drove to Spinks Airport and signed up for the Civil Air Patrol, in the very unit run by a spit-and-polish youngster from Mansfield High, David Christopher Graham. So the Southern Baptist boy and the daughter of El Templo de Juan met at last, kids with nothing in common except that both were unhappy at home. Sparks flew during their initial encounters, and their overall relationship was destined to be a stormy one.

# 7

So much did their enlistment in the Civil Air Patrol affect David and Diane's relationship and, eventually, their plot to murder Adrianne Jones, that some description of the CAP is of benefit here. Most citizens, when questioned about the Civil Air Patrol, will answer that they "have heard of it." The fact is, it is a military offshoot that has long since outlived its usefulness.

The Civil Air Patrol had its genesis during World War II, and originally was a good idea. With most able-bodied men either in the Pacific or the European theaters, defense of our shores and airspace was a point of real concern, so Congress authorized funding for a much needed volunteer unit. The Civil Air Patrol, a division of the Army Air Corps—and later incorporated into the United States Air Force once that branch of the service came into being in 1950—had its inaugural flight in 1942. Manned entirely by unpaid citizens—except for the officers required to supervise activities—CAP planes cruised the skies, keeping lookout overhead for the balance of the war. In every U.S. city were Civil Air Patrol air raid wardens, men in steel hats who conducted drills in offices, factories, and schools. Since the volunteers served without compensation, the tax dollars spent on planes for the CAP to fly were considered well worth the money at the time.

Today the official function of the Civil Air Patrol is to conduct search-and-rescue missions. Anyone whose plane is downed in the wilderness, for instance, can radio for help, at which time the volunteer forces will spring into action. The theory is sound enough, but since all of their functions overlap with duties of sheriffs, police, fire departments, or private detective agencies— and since very few people are aware of the CAP's function and wouldn't know to call the CAP should disaster strike—the Civil Air Patrol never actually rescues anyone. Instead, at the various airfields around the country where CAP squadrons are stationed—complete with uniforms, military provisions, and airplanes furnished at taxpayers' expense—men in their fifties and sixties meet one night a week to ride herd on the junior troops recruited from local high schools. And, one weekend a month, these volunteers climb into cockpits and fly around.

The junior troops are also throwbacks to World

War II, when patriotic teens too young for combat duty spent nights and weekends assisting air raid wardens. Continuation of the junior units in peacetime was considered good for Air Force recruiting purposes, so interested teens can still enlist in the CAP, attend the weekend meetings, ride once a month in airplanes, drill in formation and study military strategy, though this training—except for the plane rides—is a duplication of high school ROTC. There is a small fee for enlistment, and occasionally junior recruits have to buy belt buckles and brass that the Air Force doesn't provide. At the time Diane Zamora joined the Civil Air Patrol, the fee was thirty-five dollars.

A raw recruit begins a career in the Civil Air Patrol with one stripe on his or her uniform sleeve. Over time, passing a series of aerospace tests, and from recommendations from senior officers, it is possible to advance to the rank of cadet colonel (eleven stripes). Only cadet colonels are eligible for service academy appointments, and so rare is it for a junior CAP to reach that level, few of the nationally allotted nine appointments are ever filled.

David Graham not only commanded the junior squadron, with little supervision from the adult officers, he had already achieved ten stripes by the time he was a high school junior. He made cadet colonel a month after his senior year began, and by the time he graduated he had more medals than any cadet in the history of the Civil Air Patrol. David's appointment to the Air Force Academy came as a result of his participation in the CAP.

Diane didn't even come close. She never advanced beyond four-stripes, and, for their first three years in the unit anyway, her lack of military skills caused a lot of friction between her and David Graham. She was repeatedly late for meetings and out of step during marching drills. David was constantly on her case over her shortcomings. In retrospect, it's likely that his outward dislike for Diane was a cover for his attraction to her, but more than once she left the meetings in tears as a result of his dressing her down. She confided to other cadets that she couldn't stand David Graham, and that if not for her determination to secure an academy appointment, she would have quit the unit because of him.

After meetings the cadets often gathered at the Dairy Queen or scored a six-pack of beer and went joy riding, and occasionally one of the other cadets would invite Diane to go along. When that happened, David would hang out with B. C. Horne and his other buddies, and avoid Diane like the plague. Diane, on the other hand, would ignore the tall boy from Mansfield, talking quietly to the other girls on hand and treating the males as if they didn't exist. She coined a phrase for David, and for the balance of their tours he was known by the Spanish-speaking cadets as "*El Jefe Grande quien no sabe mierda*" (the Big Boss who doesn't know shit).

To be fair, David didn't treat Diane much differently than he did the other girls in Civil Air Patrol. The word among the female CAP cadets was that David hated women, and a few even hinted that he was gay. Nothing could be further from the truth; David's outward aversion to females was likely the result of raging hormones. Up to that point he'd been awkward and ill at ease around girls, seldom dating, and the only times he felt really confident was when leading cadets in military drills.

So it was that Diane and David went through most of their time together in Civil Air Patrol on less than friendly terms, and by the time the summer between their junior and senior years rolled around, the two were barely speaking to each other. But events were to occur that summer that altered David's attitude toward girls in general and Diane Zamora in particular.

The South Fort Worth squadron of the Civil Air Patrol went on maneuvers in Canada that summer, and as leader of the junior troops David Graham was invited along. The maneuvers included CAP counterparts from several foreign countries, and the purpose of the gathering was to compare the various methods of conducting search-and-rescue missions, and to perform a series of simulated drills. David and several other cadets flew north in the crew section of a military cargo plane, with two of the squadron's senior officers piloting the aircraft.

Canadian summers are very pleasant, daytime temperatures hovering in the mid-seventies, and the maneuvers were conducted in the majestic, snow-capped Rocky Mountains. The search-and-rescue units spent their daytimes conducting practice missions. One group of cadets would pretend to be lost in the mountains while the rest of the units used planes and ground crews to track them down. In the evenings the gathered teenagers would party and play. In Canada, for the first time in his life, David Graham found himself in demand among the ladies.

He had always been an outcast. During his middle school years—largely due to his lack of aggression on the football field—he'd developed a reputation among his classmates as a dork, and his participation in ROTC—which caused many to refer to David as a "rotsy queer"—had carried that image on into high school. Adolescents tend to categorize their peers, and once a kid is fitted into a slot it's difficult to change their minds. By the time he was a junior, David had filled out and grown into a handsome young man, and there were no doubt plenty of girls at Mansfield High who would have liked to get to know him better if they hadn't been afraid of criticism from their friends.

Intelligent and sensitive, David had reacted by withdrawing into a cocoon, and only in areas where he excelled—in military situations—did he exhibit any self-confidence at all. In fact, it was likely his feeling of inferiority that caused him to become somewhat of a tyrant to his underlings in ROTC and Civil Air Patrol.

But in Canada that summer, the scenario was quite different. The foreign units in attendance were loaded with females from France, England, and Canada who'd never heard of Mansfield High and didn't know that David was supposed to be a dork. In their eyes, David was a hero who had set records in the Civil Air Patrol, who commandeered his unit with an air of authority, and who knew more about aerospace, military strategy, and search-and-rescue technique than all the other cadets combined. These impressionable young women regarded David with the same reverence as the cheerleaders at Mansfield High regarded the captain of the football team.

### Close-up

This youngster's name is Alton Ruiz. He's a year behind Diane and David in school, lives in Joshua, and still attends Crowley High. It was at Diane's suggestion that Alton first enlisted in Civil Air Patrol when he was a sophomore. He has no college aspirations, and plans to enlist in the Air Force the day he graduates.

"Now, that David," Alton says, "was one weird dude. And after that time he went to Canada, man, the dude was even weirder."

"Weirder how?" the interviewer asks.

"Like he wasn't even the same guy. Before, he was the biggest pain in the ass with all that Air Force and shit."

"I thought everybody in Civil Air Patrol was interested in the Air Force."

Alton cuts his eyes in the interviewer's direction and digs in the breast pocket of his fatigues for a pack of Salems. "Look, man, I come out here 'cause I wanna be in the Air Force. It's gonna be my life, but I got no delusions. It's better than going out to Grand Prairie and driving rivets in the factory. But that David, he thought he was some kinda Stormin' Norman or somebody. That's what some of 'em called the dude, Stormin' Norman Graham. Went around wanting everybody to call him 'sir' and shit."

"And after Canada, he no longer did?"

"Oh, he still come to meetings with his nose in the air, all right, but it was like he was one of the regular guys sometimes. Sat around telling us how he got all this pussy up in Canada, told them same stories over and over till we got kinda sick of listening to the dude."

"He had some sexual encounters up there?"

Alton snorts derisively. "To hear him tell it, every night."

"You sound like you didn't like David very much."

"Hell, would you? Nobody likes him now, after he and Diane got into all that shit, but I never cared much for the dude to begin with. Sitting around talking about all these women he had up there, said it so much I thought he probably bull-shitting some."

"He named names and gave details, huh?" the interviewer says.

"Talked about two of 'em, mostly, this English girl and this Canadian girl. Said they done anything he wanted 'em to, like he's the only dude ever had a piece of ass."

"It was after that Canadian trip that he and Diane started going together, wasn't it?"

Alton lights a smoke and inhales, his jaw thrusting out in a pugnacious attitude. "I talked to him about that."

"About going with Diane?"

Alton nods. "He started hitting on her that summer, after he got back off that trip. Up to then he was on her ass all the time about marching and shit, but first thing you know the dude's hitting on her. Now, I never had nothing with Diane, don't get me wrong, but we were pretty good friends. I thought David was just trying to get in her pants, and I needed to set him straight about Spanish girls."

"That they're different somehow?" the interviewer says.

"Diane come on giggling a lot and acting silly, like she might be somebody the dude could screw pretty easy. But she wasn't like that, not at all. I mean, Diane was a virgin. I just thought if he was looking for something like that, somebody needed to tell him he was hitting on the wrong chick."

"Did you talk to him?"

Alton cracks his window open to let the smoke out of the car. "Tried to. He told me it wasn't none of my business, and that he really thought she was special. I didn't believe him and still thought he was only trying to score with her, but the next thing you know they were all in love and shit."

The interviewer makes a note. "So you'd say, after Canada, David changed a lot."

Alton is silent for a moment. "Before he went up there," he finally says, "it was like he didn't know there was any difference between little boys and little girls. Thought one trooper was just like another, you know? But after Canada, man, *shsh*. Turned him into a stone pussy freak, is what it done."

Ever since she'd learned about her father's affair, Diane's demeanor had changed as well, though the alteration in her personality was gradual whereas the changes in David seemed to come overnight. Previously she'd been on the shy side, but she had slowly developed feistiness. No longer did she accept criticism in the CAP unit with her head down and her gaze on the floor; now she would look her adversary straight in the eye and answer back.

Not that her performance in Civil Air Patrol had improved; she continued to come in late and screw up in drills. But now when asked why she'd fouled up, she was apt to reply, "Because I felt like it." While David was away in Canada, Diane got into a screaming match with one of the senior officers over her rumpled uniform. The older man tried to reason with her in vain, then finally threw up his hands in disgust and walked away.

Most cadets in the unit, including Alton Ruiz, thought that sparks would fly on David's return. David had never been one to put up with guff from his troops, and they expected his back to arch like an alleycat's the first time Cadet Zamora talked back to him. As David confronted his underlings on his first evening back from Canada, the unit collectively held its breath. They were to be sorely disappointed.

An inspection was scheduled that night, preceded by a marching drill. During the first segment Diane's marching was even worse than usual, and as inspection began her uniform was in disarray. But to his troops' amazement, David ignored her shortcomings. When he stopped to give Cadet Zamora the once-over, he simply grinned at her without comment, and she returned his look with a twinkle in her eye. The cadet troop began to wonder what was going on.

It didn't take them long to find out. One night about a week after David returned from Canada, the CAP cadets rendezvoused in Chili's Restaurant after their meeting. Diane rode to Chili's along with two other girls. The group was already seated and had placed their orders when David strode in from the parking lot. Some of the guys scooted over in a booth to make room for him, but instead of taking his accustomed seat, David walked right past them and squeezed in alongside Diane Zamora.

All during the meal, Diane and David sat close to each other and spoke in soft tones, exchanging looks and ignoring everyone else in the room. The others felt uncomfortable, eating their chili-cheeseburgers and leaving the restaurant in a hurry. Before long, the group at Chili's had dwindled down to David, Diane, Alton Ruiz, and a couple of other guys.

As Alton and his pals looked the other way and pretended not to notice, David would gather up both his and Diane's checks and pay the waitress. Then he'd take Diane's arm and steer her toward the exit, passing the boys' table without so much as speaking to them. As David and Diane reached the door and went through it into the parking lot, they were holding hands. As David's pickup went by the window and pulled out into the street, Diane was sitting close by David's side.

Just about everyone close to the Adrianne Jones murder case—newspaper and magazine writers, police, prosecutors, defense attorneys, and family and friends of the tragic couple—has a theory as to what caused David and Diane eventually to go off the deep end. In David's case, many point to the abruptness of his parents' separation. Janice Graham left her husband without warning, leaving a note on the kitchen table to the effect that she couldn't live with Jerry any longer because he refused to discipline David—and David was first to find the note on coming home from school. There isn't any doubt that the rift between his mother and father had an adverse effect on the boy, but David was a problem long before that. In the months before Janice left, he'd stolen his father's credit card, charged several thousand dollars worth of stereo equipment, then screamed defiantly in his parents' faces when confronted over the incident. His behavior had gone downhill ever since middle school, and analyzing David's decline doesn't require a psychologist. He was a terribly unhappy, socially misfit young man, and his transgressions were really nothing more than a cry for attention. Regardless of his initial motives in pursuing Diane, that summer she became his first true love. As anyone who has experienced passion as a teenager will testify, falling in love will make a kid do some ridiculous things, and David's lack of experience with girls up to that time made him even more susceptible.

Diane's participation in the murder is more of a puzzle, even though there is her father's affair to use as a reference point. Until her involvement with David, Diane's family says that she was a model child, and it's the consensus among the Zamora clan that it was David who led her astray. All of her aunts and uncles describe her as being "obsessed" with David, and say that when they were together she clung desperately to him and shut her family out.

David's kin, understandably, feel that it was the other way around, that he was "obsessed" with her, and that if it hadn't been for the girl from South Fort Worth, David would be well on his way to a successful Air Force career.

The families' animosity toward each other is one reason for the volatility of David and Diane's passion for each other. David's folks didn't like Diane, and Diane's folks didn't like David. The more their families tried to drive them apart, the more they were determined to stay together. Additionally, family opposition went deeper than mere judgment that David was bad for Diane or Diane was bad for David. Painful though it may be, there is a never-before-discussed aspect of differences between the Grahams and Zamoras that should be an open topic in any analysis of David and Diane's crime.

America's politically correct media has bent over backward to keep from bringing up the racial difference between them, but the difference can't be ignored. Black-and-white conflict draws the most public attention, but in Texas the racism between Anglos and Hispanics is every bit as severe. Mexican immigrants in Texas received the same shabby treatment as did Jews and Italians in nineteenth-century New York, and the resentment of the immigrants' descendants is understandable. So, while David and Diane didn't consider their racial difference a barrier to their relationship, their parents almost certainly did.

All of this would have affected Diane in certain ways. Growing up in a Hispanic community—and being a student from the poorer area bused in to Crowley High—would have made her acutely aware of Anglos' superior position in the social structure. While the ethnic difference didn't keep her from falling head over heels for David, race would have been a factor in her evaluation of any competitor for his affections. Anglo girls had all the advantages, and any Anglo female trespassing on Diane's turf would be more of a threat.

Once David and Diane connected, they were together day and night for the balance of the summer. David forsook his male friends altogether; whereas previously he was always ready for late-night beer-drinking jaunts with B. C. Horne or other pals, now when Diane couldn't be out for one reason or the other, David stayed at home to talk to her on the phone. Teenlike, they developed pet names for each other—she was his angel, he was her *hombre mucho*—and code words to convey their feelings when adults might be listening in. These code messages could get pretty silly: One was "drab green female sheep," which loosely translates to olive (I love) ewe. Even on occasions when they would go places with other kids, the others were made to feel like outsiders. When a vanful of adolescents rode up to the Dairy Queen, David and Diane would stay in the car, making out. Previously David's one passion in life had been the military, but he and Diane got to the point where they even groped at each other during Civil Air Patrol meetings.

"Man, it was ridiculous," Alton Ruiz says. "I'll say this for the dude, he used to be a helluva soldier. But once him and Diane started getting it on, it was like the rest of the unit could go to hell. Inspections used to be a bitch with that David doing 'em, but once they were all in love and shit, we could have come in naked and he wouldn't have noticed. They'd stand up to each other and she'd have her tits up against him, and it wouldn't have surprised any of us if they'd gone to doing it right there in the squadron room."

David even went to South Fort Worth a few times and attended El Templo de Juan with Diane, even though he understood little Spanish and had to depend on her to translate for him. During these visits the Zamora clan had their first look at him and, aunt-and-uncle-like, gossipped among themselves about Diane's new boyfriend. The consensus was that David was very controlling with Diane, and the family was worried that he stood between her and them. On being introduced to members of Diane's family, David had little to say, returning their greetings with a series of grunts and refusing to look any of them in the eye.

Most of the Zamoras' friends and neighbors since Diane's arrest have sided with the Zamora clan. They feel that David was distant and unfriendly. Lorena Jordan lived down the street and often baby-sat the Zamoras' younger kids while Carlos and Gloria were at work. One day David showed up at Lorena's door and, as Diane stayed outside in David's pickup, told Lorena he was there to pick up Diane's younger sister. "Didn't introduce himself or anything," Lorena says. "Just stands out on the porch and tells me he's there for the baby. I wasn't about to turn the child over to just anybody, and when I asked who he was, he just told me, 'Diane's out in the car if you want to ask her.' I went out there and told Diane that she should have come to the door instead of him, and all the while he just stood there looking off. I'm telling you, that young man was weird."

Yet it's hard to know how much weight these observations should be given. All teens are self-conscious, and that David, when thrust among total strangers—not to mention people from a wholly different ethnic social structure—was less than a witty conversationalist is not at all surprising. Teenagers often fail to introduce themselves to friends' parents or so much as speak to adults. The same holds true with those in David's camp who feel that Diane was the controller. She couldn't be expected to be comfortable around David's folks any more than he was comfortable with hers.

A better way to see the potential for trouble ahead is to talk to other kids, because it is only in the company of peers that adolescents' true personalities show through. And all during that summer and the following autumn, Diane and David did things that even their cohorts who played in the wee small hours didn't understand. Among them there is little surprise that David

Graham and Diane Zamora were a couple of powder kegs, just waiting to blow sky-high.

*Close-up*

The couple sit side by side on a couch with cotton stuffing poking out, in a tiny garage apartment in Irving just a stone's throw from Texas Stadium. Their names are Regina and Stan; he's black and she is white, and she is eight months pregnant. She dropped out of Mansfield High in the spring, when she discovered that she was going to have a baby, and she hasn't seen her parents since she and Stan moved in together. She's eighteen and Stan is twenty-four. They met a year and a half ago, when Stan was out of work and got by selling drugs and whiskey to high school students in Mansfield and Cedar Hill. David Graham was a regular liquor customer, and sometimes brought Diane Zamora along with him to make a buy.

"I never saw anybody drink the way he did," Stan says. "Sometime he'd get one bottle along about eight o'clock in the evening, and then come back for another one before midnight."

"And he wouldn't be drunk?" the interviewer says.

"He was a person, it be hard to tell," Stan says. "Sometime maybe he stagger a little bit, but he speak real clear when he tell what he was after."

"What about the girl? Diane. Would she be drinking, too?"

"She always stay in the car. Other than seeing her with him I didn't know this chick, but she's the same one I seen her picture in the paper."

"When they were arrested?" the interviewer asks.

Stan nods and, as Regina pats his leg, pushes her hand aside. "I never knew him too good, either, only to sell him stuff. Gina and this other dude brought 'em to me."

The interviewer looks to the girl. "A friend of yours?"

Regina shifts uncomfortably and folds her arms over her bulbous abdomen. "This guy Carl," she says, "him and David were in ROTC. They heard I could score some booze and asked me about it at school."

"Did Diane and David ever buy any drugs?" the interviewer says.

Stan frowns, thinking this one over. "Maybe some uppers a couple of times, but not much. If he bought toot or anything he was getting it for her, 'cause he was a dude that was too far into alcohol."

The interviewer turns a page in his spiral notepad. "Did David ever act violent when he was drinking?"

"I don't know nothing about that," Stan says.

"Only times I ever saw him was on a road out by the lake, when he'd meet me."

The interviewer turns once again to the girl. "How about you?"

"I don't know about violent. They yelled at each other some, being jealous," Regina says.

"Oh? Jealous of who?"

"Of anybody. If he thought she was looking at some other guy or she thought he was interested in some other chick, they'd scream so loud you could hear 'em for miles. One night outside the Pizza Inn where I was working, he got really pissed and drove off and left her in the parking lot. She came in and used the phone, but first thing you know he came back and picked her up. Squealed out of the parking lot on two wheels, like that pickup truck was about to turn over. He drove pretty crazy."

"And that night," the interviewer says. "Had David been drinking?"

Regina and Stan share a grin. Finally she says, swinging her foot, "Oh, yeah, he'd been drinking. Any time you saw David Graham out late at night, that's one thing you could count on."

Diane and David decided before the summer was over that they wanted to get married, but withheld their announcement until just before Christmas so that their wedding plans wouldn't affect their service academy appointments. Antidiscrimination laws don't permit rejection from the military schools due to marital status; nonetheless, married applicants often learn after the fact that their papers were somehow lost in the shuffle.

As the beginning of their senior year in high school drew closer, David encouraged Diane to get in physical shape. Regardless of which service academy the couple attended, the early months were going to be an ordeal. While they continued to carouse and drink almost every night, the lovers began to meet at the Mansfield High School track in the afternoon prior to Civil Air Patrol for a run. David was in good condition, but Diane was not, and at his urging she agreed, once the fall term began, to sign up for the cross-country team. So determined was Diane to attend a service academy that she was willing to go through any torture to improve her chances of success, but she confided to friends that she despised working out with a passion, and decided very quickly that participation in cross-country could kill someone.

# 8

Media reports concerning Adrianne Jones's murder tout David as a gifted scholar and above-average athlete, but he wasn't any more of a star in cross-country than he had been in football. To complete his high school graduation requirements he was faced with a choice. Participation in athletics counted a quarter-credit per year, as did choir, band, art, or dance class, and a couple of hours running to stay in shape every day seemed the lesser evil of the five. To David's credit he did stick with running throughout high school, though he was never included in the top fifteen on the squad who competed in dual meets. The entire team runs in district and regional events, held in November at the close of the cross-country season, and an examination of regional meet records from 1991 through 1995 shows nary a point for Mansfield High School scored by David Graham.

Cross-country workouts at Mansfield High

David Graham and Diane Zamora, honor students and
service academy appointees, seemed an ideal teen
couple until they were linked to the murder
of Adrianne Jones (*below*).

David, shown here drilling his Mansfield High ROTC troops, went on to the Air Force Academy and made it through the hell of induction summer with flying colors.

Though she hated running, Diane tried out for the Crowley High cross-country team at David's urging. (*Photo courtesy of the Zamora family*)

Adrianne worked her last shift at the Golden Chicken on the afternoon of her death. (*Photo by Greg Gray*)

The Jones family home (*above*) and the isolated spot (*below*) where Adrianne's body was found. (*Photos by Carlton Stowers*)

Adrianne's mother, Linda Jones, at the site of a tree planting in memory of her daughter. (*Photo by Greg Ellman*/Ft. Worth Star Telegram/*SIPA Press*)

While Adrianne's friends and family mourned, David and Diane happily helped each other pack for their first year at the academies. (*Photo by Robert Rule*/Ft. Worth Star Telegram/*SIPA Press*)

Diane salutes with fellow first-year plebe, Jay Guild. Jay kept his silence after Diane confided in him, and as a result had to leave the academy. Note the position of Diane's injured left hand compared with the position of Jay's left hand. (*Photo courtesy of the Zamora family*)

David Graham's high-profile Houston attorney, Dan Cogdell, plans a double-barrelled attack on the admissibility of David's confession.

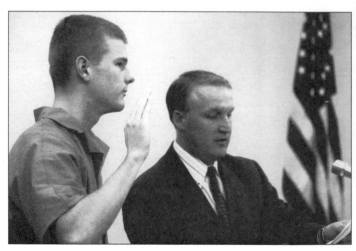

David with lawyer Bob Swofford, Cogdell's chief assistant, appearing at David's extradition hearing in Colorado Springs. (*Photo by Bob Jackson/Colorado Springs* Gazette Telegraph)

Judge Drago has the charge of ensuring a fair trial despite the media circus surrounding the case. (*Photo by Pat Stowers*)

Diane Zamora enters court, followed closely by a guard on the day of her civil hearing. (*Photo by Pat Stowers*)

Defense lawyer John Linebarger continues to fiercely represent Diane despite her family's inability to pay his fee. (*Photo by Pat Stowers*)

Diane's parents, Carlos and Gloria (*second and third from the left*), with other family members at the civil hearing in which they lost their attempt to block the airing of a television movie about the case. (*Photo by Pat Stowers*)

begin at seven-thirty in the morning and extend through the first school period of the day, and male and female runners share the track and take laps together. Adrianne Jones was one of the top runners on the girls' team, though as a sophomore she competed on the junior varsity. While David's position on the boys' varsity was one of obscurity, everyone who participated in cross-country running at Mansfield High remembers Adrianne well.

*Close-up*

"Hell, yes, her," the straw-haired youngster says. "Who could forget?"

"She was pretty fast, eh?" the interviewer says.

"Who cared? We'd sort of lag behind doing laps and then fall in behind her."

The interviewer chuckles. "She had assets other than speed?"

"Are you kidding? Ass that wouldn't quit."

The scene is a service station bay at the eastern edge of Mansfield, and this boy's name is Wilson James. He is wiry and prominent veined, and wears a gray work uniform with his name stitched over the right breast pocket.

"How well did you know Adrianne?" the interviewer says.

"She was the type, everybody knew. Talked to everybody, was really sweet. And, man, good-looking."

"You ran cross-country every year?"

"Yeah, it was something to do," he says.

"Then you knew David, too."

"He was in my class. We weren't asshole buddies, but yeah. I knew him, yeah."

"What I'm trying to get a handle on," the interviewer says, "is this relationship he was supposed to have had with Adrianne."

"What relationship?" Wilson says.

"This sexual tryst, in his confession."

"You mean, about him fucking her?"

"Sure, the articles—"

"I read all that. If that's what he says he did, it's what he says."

The interviewer snaps open his briefcase and brandishes a *People* magazine with Adrianne's glamour shot on the cover. "This what you mean?"

"That. All those newspapers. You won't find anybody around town, hadn't read all that stuff. Him saying it and him doing it, it's two different things."

The interviewer glances at the text in the article. "After a team cross-country trip."

"I was on that trip." Wilson shows a curt nod as he wipes off his hands.

"That's the reason I wanted to talk to you. I heard that you were. How did they act?"

"How did who act?"

"Adrianne and David."

"Like everybody else, I guess. They ran in the meet."

"Were they friendly?"

Wilson puts hands on hips and looks over his shoulder. "I can't say. Nobody else can say."

"They didn't attract much attention on the trip?"

"*She* did. She always did."

"What about him?"

"He was along on the trip, if that's what you're asking."

"Did they eat together, hang out . . . ?"

"I really can't say," Wilson says.

"You can't say," the interviewer says, "or you don't want to say?"

Wilson gives a sigh of resignation. "We rode from here to Lubbock in vans and cars and spent one night in a motel. If he was hitting on Adrianne or she was hitting on him, I don't remember it. Tell the truth, I don't even think they rode in the same van."

"What about, when you came back from the meet? Didn't David and Adrianne go off together?"

Wilson regards the interviewer with a deadpan look. "No," he says.

"How can you be sure of that?"

Wilson looks thoughtful. "Okay, I'll change that to, no, I don't think so."

"You sound like you don't think David was telling the truth in his confession."

Wilson arches an eyebrow. "I do?"

"Sure, it's what he told Diane Zamora, and that's what supposedly set the whole thing off."

Wilson carries a new filter up under the truck. "I know that's what he told his girlfriend, and I know they're saying, that's why she got killed."

"But you don't buy it?"

Wilson flashes a tiny grin. "I buy it that, he told that to his girlfriend."

"If I'm understanding you right," the interviewer says, "then you think he might've been lying to her about the whole thing."

The grin broadens. "Might've?"

"Then you don't believe David's story at all."

"I don't want to get mixed up in all this."

"I'm just asking what you saw," the interviewer says.

"Yeah, okay," Wilson says. "We went on a cross-country trip. He went, she went. We come back to the high school, late at night. Me, and nobody I ever talked to, none of us remembers him and her going off together. Much as those chicks keep their noses in each other's business, you'd think one of 'em would remember that, right?"

"I've got to admit," the interviewer says, "one would think so."

"So all I can say," Wilson says, "is that both of

'em went on that trip. I never saw him talking to her, or her talking to him, and neither did anybody else I know, and that's all you're going to get from me. As for David Graham taking Adrianne Jones out and doing it to her or something, as far as I'm concerned, that's just what *he* says."

So goes the feeling among many of David's cross-country teammates. In the weeks after the arrest, newspaper, magazine, and television reporters descended on Mansfield like locusts, interviewing everyone who professed the tiniest bit of knowledge about the case, and while many conflicting reports hit the wires, one factor remains common today. Not a single member of the Mansfield High School cross-country team— at least among those willing to say anything at all—recalls any contact between David and Adrianne, either on the trip to Lubbock or afterward. Many students expressed surprise that the outgoing blond sophomore and the senior ROTC commandant were ever more than passing acquaintances. Much of what happened is a matter of public record, but the description of the one hot night of passion that has captured the public eye is an undocumented tale from David and him alone. It is an ironic but definite possibility that the catalyst in the entire case, the tryst that sent Diane Zamora into a murderous rage that culminated in Adrianne Jones's death, never really happened at all.

A crucial traffic mishap Diane suffered was a real event, one that concerns whether she could have participated in the murder. The accident occurred on a twisting road outside Mansfield after David allowed Diane to drive his pickup home. It had been raining and the pavement was slick, and Diane went into a terrible skid. The pickup spun around several times, tilted, rolled over twice, and came to a halt on its roof with Diane hanging upside down by her seatbelt. The passenger side caved in and caught Diane's upper left arm between the steering wheel, door, and twisting dashboard. In the crush her hand was mashed into a bloody pulp. A lone motorist happened along, punched 911 into his cell phone, and waited for the ambulance to arrive. The traffic crews cut the semiconscious Diane out of the cab with a blowtorch and loaded her into the ambulance, which then rushed off to the hospital with its siren wailing.

Just why David permitted the love of his life to take his car isn't clear. And why Diane wasn't driving in a safe manner remains a mystery as well. Because of the critical nature of Diane's injury and the haste of the medics to rush her in for medical attention, police on the scene deviated from the norm and dispensed with the usual breathalyzer test.

The Zamora family drew one lucky break: Gloria was working two jobs at the time, and Diane had coverage under an HMO. The insurance permitted her to avoid the county hospital, and thus she received better-than-average surgical repair. Diane's mangled hand went under the knife three different times, and the surgeons performed a mini-miracle. At the time she checked into the hospital after the accident, her left little finger hung by a thread of skin, and there was talk of amputating her ring and middle fingers as well. The surgery involved tendon splicing and grafting of skin from her hip, so that today the hand looks normal at a glance. A closer inspection, however, reveals that the last three fingers remained curled at all times, and that Diane performs almost all tasks with her right hand while the left rests lifelessly in her lap or on her thigh. Her application to the Naval Academy was already in before the accident, so she didn't fudge as to her physical impairments, but flight school would have been out of the question had she remained in the service. What she might have done in a towering fit of rage is unknown, but the fact remains that she is barely able to lift a glass of water to her lips with the left hand.

The wreck left David without wheels, but he managed to borrow his father's car to visit the hospital every day while Diane was a patient, sitting quietly in a chair alongside her bed and doing his homework while she watched TV. Diane missed a great deal of school as a result of her surgeries, and worried constantly about her college plans. If not for special considerations granted in her case, she wouldn't have graduated from high school on time.

As Diane's health improved and she spent more and more time away from the hospital, she found herself without transportation as well. Sympathetic to his daughter's plight, Carlos made one more trip to a used-car lot and bought Diane a Mazda hatchback. This solved her problem, though the car was a bit cramped inside and David had to incline his neck to keep from bumping his head on the ceiling when she took him for a ride. Like the strength remaining in Diane's left hand, the amount of room inside the Mazda became a factor on that terrible night.

While Diane was temporarily out of circulation, David returned his attention to ROTC and Civil Air Patrol meetings. He didn't miss many days visiting Diane, either at home or at the hospital, but he focused on the military a great deal more than he had during the summer. His rejuvenated interest affected the cadets as a whole, and by mid-semester his ROTC unit's marching was as sharp as it had ever been.

Even as his participation in the military improved, though, his attendance at cross-country workouts became sporadic. Rules are lax in athletics classes for high school seniors, particularly those not considered cogs of the team, and the coaches overlooked the fact that David was late for practice on many days. He had a legitimate excuse. He was worried about Diane and checked on her often, and most of the time when he missed part or all of a workout he was on the phone with her. He was absent on team picture day, so wasn't featured on the cross-country team in his senior annual, and even when the squad qualified for the regional meet in Lubbock he told some of his teammates that he didn't think he'd go on the trip. The team would travel most of the day on a Friday and wouldn't return until late on Saturday night, and David couldn't bear the thought of an entire weekend away from his steady. Diane, however, learned at the last minute that she wouldn't be able to see him that weekend because of some church commitments. So David changed his mind at the last minute, and when a gang of excited youngsters piled into cars and vans for the day-long trip across the West Texas prairie, David Graham rode along with the rest of the team.

There is no long haul like a ride through West Texas. The old saw is that it's the only place in the world where you can drive for miles and miles and see nothing but miles and miles. The terrain is flat and stretches into the distance like a moonscape, with only an occasional mesquite tree or tumbleweed to break the monotony.

It's a seven-hour ride from Mansfield to Lubbock. November weather in the Lone Star State is still plenty warm, and the temperature on November 3 in Mansfield touched the lower eighties. The caravan left Mansfield High just after lunch and didn't arrive at the motel in Lubbock until after dark and, curfews aside, it was well into the morning hours before the chaperones could get the pumped-up teens into bed.

The Mansfield Tigers didn't do particularly well in the meet. There were a couple of high finishers on the squad, but the overall times were poor. The girls' j.v. fared much better than any of the varsity teams, and Adrianne Jones jogged across the finish line with one of the better clockings. After times were posted and trophies awarded, the team from Mansfield piled back into the cars and vans for the long trip home.

Since David is the only one left to tell the tale, we must let him take it from here. According to him, Adrianne grew more and more friendly on the ride home, and by the time the caravan arrived at the Mansfield High parking lot around midnight, she was practically in David's lap in the back of the van. Then, as the group hauled tote bags and overnight cases from trunk and tailgate, she asked David if he'd mind giving her a ride home. Ever the gentleman, David agreed, and the two—hauling their luggage amid a group of teenagers through the parking lot—made their way to David's father's car and drove off into the night without anyone—chaperones, coaches, teammates both male and female—noticing.

The drive from the high school to Adrianne's house is a short one. On the way, Adrianne allegedly directed David to the parking lot behind "an elementary school"—Alice Ponder Elementary School is the only grade school the couple would pass along the way—where Adrianne took the offensive and they had sex. Then David took Adrianne home, and sped off through the night to call Diane and tell her how much he'd missed her while he was gone.

There are other aspects of the story that give one pause as well. Adrianne ran in a group where the girls weren't a bit shy in detailing their sexual experiences to each other. In the weeks prior to her death, she went on and on to her friends about her late-night adventures with Tracy Smith, her lack of interest in James Drummond, and told freely of sneaking out of the house to go as far away as Denton—about fifty miles—to attend all-night drinking and drug parties at apartments of North Texas University students. Yet nowhere in all this chitchat was there any mention of any involvement with David Graham. Additionally, after the alleged incident David and Adrianne—outwardly anyway—didn't seem any better acquainted than before the cross-country trip, at least to those who knew them both. So while David's tale may be true—though his professed lack of aggression in the incident seems exaggerated—it's just as possible that the sexual encounter was a made-up story.

Whether his having sex with Adrianne Jones was real or imagined, David couldn't have expected the reaction he got from Diane when he told her about it. His motive for confessing isn't clear. David says he was grief-stricken over being unfaithful, but Diane has told others that he was bragging during a lovers' spat. Nor is the exact time when his conscience got the better of him.

In his murder confession David said he told Diane on the very same night that the incident occurred, and that the plot to kill Adrianne hatched from there. According to the document David dictated and signed for detectives at the Air Force Academy, he and Diane first planned to do Adrianne in on the night of November 5—the night after the team returned from Lubbock—but when he called her to lure her to her death, she wasn't home. Since then, however, he has said to jail visitors and personnel that it was nearly a month after his encounter with Adrianne until he told Diane. Diane's own murder confession doesn't specify when she found out about David and Adrianne, but the imprisoned lovers' descriptions of her reaction are almost identical.

Diane was livid, and her anger was directed, not at David but at Adrianne. Assuming that his description to Diane of the event was the same as he told in his confession—that Adrianne was the aggressor and lured him into the parking lot—Diane's feelings are not all that surprising. She had never met Adrianne Jones, and until David told her the story had never even heard of the girl. To Diane's way of thinking, Adrianne had invaded her turf and had sex with her boyfriend, and for that the blonde would have to pay. So while Diane's venom toward Adrianne seems a natural reaction, her plan for revenge was more bizarre than any fiction writer could possibly imagine.

After a bout of hysterical sobbing, Diane turned to David and said, her voice trembling, "You've got to kill her, David." (This is a direct quote from David's confession, backed by Diane's own statement to police, incredible as it seems.)

David was stunned and didn't answer.

"If you love me, you'll do it."

"I do love you," David said. "But . . . *kill* her?"

"Yes. Kill the bitch."

"Kill her how, Diane? You don't know what you're saying."

"I know exactly what I'm saying, and I want you to do it."

"You want me to kill her?"

"Kill the bitch. Kill her dead."

It is interesting to note that everything Diane confessed about the murder mirrors to the minutest detail what David tells in his own confession, which is odd in itself. Veterans of police investigation say that it is extremely rare for dual perpetrators of a grisly crime to remember details exactly alike. The overall descriptions will be the same, but suspects' memories of the precise order of events—there is, after all, a lot going on during the commission of a homicide—will contain discrepancies. But in Diane and David's case, their recollections of the killing are exactly alike, as if they'd memorized a script and recited it word for word.

# 9

Detectives Dennis Meyer and Dennis Clay have received a lot of flak over their investigation into the death of Adrianne Jones, but it is also true that the detectives were under massive heat from the day that Adrianne died. Even though the murder didn't make a ripple nationally for months, it was a prominent feature in local papers from the outset. Word came quickly down from upstairs that the case had to be cleared, and the sooner the better.

It is no secret that Grand Prairie police chief Harry Crum has political ambitions beyond his current position, and has had them for several years. The dapper chief dresses more like a gubernatorial candidate than an officer of the law, appears at all the right social functions, and regularly addresses crime-prevention associations and meetings of the Kiwanis and Rotary clubs. It was heavily rumored during 1995 that Crum would throw his hat in the ring in the next

Tarrant County sheriff's race, but since the brouhaha regarding the botched arrest in the Adrianne Jones murder, Chief Crum has all but disappeared from public view.

Following the murder, Linda Jones became almost as visible in the community as the chief himself. Frantic with grief over her daughter's death, Linda did everything possible to ensure that Adrianne wasn't forgotten. For weeks she left the lights on in Adrianne's room, as if expecting her daughter to return, and constantly attended meetings of victims' rights and mothers' groups. She made calls almost daily to Meyer and Clay, demanding to know how the investigation was proceeding, and if she didn't get satisfactory answers, she wasn't hesitant to give the detectives a piece of her mind. It became abundantly clear that if there was ever to be tranquility within the department, Adrianne's murder must be solved.

All of this pressure caused Meyer and Clay to be less than prudent in their handling of James Drummond, the high school dropout who'd failed during his initial interview to account for his whereabouts on the night of the killing, and to be less than aggressive in pursuing other suspects. Although Linda Jones asked them several times whether they'd followed up on Adrianne's call from "David in cross-country," other than a perfunctory question of David at the high school they failed to take heed. As far as Meyer and Clay were concerned, they had their man already.

Yet they had major problems in building a case against the seventeen-year-old, problems that, as veteran investigators, Clay and Meyer certainly understood. There wasn't a shred of physical evidence to tie James to the crime scene, and while he'd been vague as to his whereabouts on the night of the murder and had lied about even knowing Adrianne when first questioned, taking what they had to the district attorney's office in an effort to secure an indictment would have been a waste of time at that point. Once in custody, James might crack under the pressure and confess, but in order make an arrest Meyer and Clay would have to fudge a bit on probable cause.

By way of simplified definition, probable cause is a legal reason to arrest someone for a crime before a grand jury returns an indictment. Sometimes probable cause is obvious; if the perpetrator is climbing out a warehouse window when the cop car peels around the corner in response to a 911 call, then a burglary arrest is certainly reasonable. The same holds true when a patrolman smells marijuana smoke inside a car he's stopped for a traffic violation. Without eyewitnesses—or fingerprint evidence, or anything else that ties the suspect to the crime—probable cause becomes a gray area.

In all cases where the suspect isn't apprehended at the scene, police must get a probable-cause warrant signed by a judge before they can make an arrest. Such warrants aren't hard to get. Judges depend on policemen to know what constitutes probable cause, and in the large majority of cases, securing a warrant becomes almost a rubber-stamp procedure.

Late in the evening on December 14, 1995, Detective Dennis Clay approached a judge with a request for a warrant. Attached to the request was Clay's sworn affidavit, which read as follows: "The description of the crime scene hypothesized by the suspect is very similar to the actual crime scene." In other words, in hazarding a guess that Adrianne's body was found out by the lake, James Drummond had hit the nail on the head. By midnight, the police had their warrant and were on their way.

James Drummond's family has more ammunition in their lawsuit than the mere fact that police came out in the dead of night and arrested the boy. Since his original question-and-answer session at the police station, James and his parents had called detectives numerous times, asking how the investigation was going and offered to come in once more should police want additional information. In fairness to the detectives, it should be noted that calls from criminals who want to know if the cops are about to come down on them are common, and that police don't normally level with such callers. According to James Drummond's father, however, he'd personally asked Clay to give his son a chance to turn himself in if an arrest became imminent, and Clay had assured him that James would have that opportunity. Once again, though, criminals often make such requests only so they can go on the lam should the cops actually call them. Policemen know this and make such assurances—particularly in homicide cases—only to keep the suspect off guard. So up to the point of James's arrest, police hadn't deviated much from normal procedure. The serving of the warrant, however, was a horse of a different color.

Around one in the morning, with Meyer and Clay giving directional hand signals, riot squads and tactical units quietly surrounded the Drummond home, a modest one-story house. Then, as the tactical squad took to the roof armed with ropes and grappling hooks, and the shotgunners trained their weapons on the windows, the detectives crept onto the porch and, on a count of three, bashed in the door with a battering ram.

When the clatter arose in their living room and on the roof, James's mother and father sat bolt upright in bed. Good Lord, St. Nick and his band of reindeer weren't due for ten more days. The

Drummonds were naturally confused as to what was going on. Out of the bedroom Mr. and Mrs. Drummond came, only to have shotguns thrust in their faces. Grand Prairie's finest ordered them to sit on their sofa and keep out of the way. The couple complied, and sat trembling in terror as GPPD troops stormed into James's room. In moments the officers returned with the Drummonds' son in leg irons and handcuffs, and herded the boy out through the front with a shotgun prodding him from behind.

Even then, the ordeal wasn't over. As policemen detained the Drummonds in the living room, a group of officers entered James's room. They pulled the mattress from the bed, opened and emptied all the drawers, pulled clothing from hangers in the closet and left the garments in a pile on the floor. They then ordered the Drummonds not to go into their son's room and disturb anything—but failed to specify for what period of time the Drummonds were forbidden to move freely about in their own home. As the Drummonds stood by helplessly, a wrecker pulled into their driveway outside, hooked onto James's truck, and towed it downtown.

Suspects in criminal cases who shield their faces with their arms while entering the jailhouse are familiar sights on the evening news, but in the Graham-Zamora-Adrianne Jones case there has been a role reversal. It is the *policemen* involved who don't want anyone seeing or talking to them. Newsmen calling the Grand Prairie Police Department, identifying themselves, and then asking to speak to Meyer or Clay were put on hold and left there. If the reporter happens to play it cagey, misidentifying himself, and Meyer or Clay picks up the phone, they hang up immediately.

James Drummond, through the attorneys representing him in his lawsuit, is the only one doing any talking about his arrest, and he has plenty to say. The following is James's account of what went on while he was in jail for twenty-two days.

According to James, as soon as the GPPD brought him to their main headquarters, they fingerprinted him, took his mug-shot photo, relieved him of his valuables, then stripped him naked and locked him in a padded cell. (The padded cell is standard procedure for prisoners under suicide watch, as is removal of their clothing and the taking away of any items, such as pencils or pens, with which they might harm themselves. However, federal law prohibits such measures before an inmate has an interview with mental health officials in order to determine whether he or she is indeed suicidal, and James's records while incarcerated reflect no such interviews.) The detectives then proceeded to grill him in shifts, around the clock, for several days.

Presumably one of the interrogators was a female detective named Teena Jackson, who appears alongside Meyer and Clay as a defendant in the lawsuit.

Also according to James, police conducted these interrogations without giving him any meals—he says he didn't have a bite to eat until being transferred to the Tarrant County Jail four days after his arrest—or giving him a chance to talk to a lawyer. (To be fair, the onus isn't on the police to offer an attorney's services; rather, it is up to the suspect to ask for counsel. However, the cops are required to give Miranda warnings to all arrestees, including the prisoner's right to an attorney if he wants one. The lawsuit is silent as to whether James ever received a Miranda warning.) During these sessions James states he cowered on the floor of his cell while the detectives hovered over him, screaming and cursing.

During one particularly grueling period Detective Meyer allegedly stood menacingly over James, who was huddled shivering and stark naked in one corner. In the detective's hands was a picture of Adrianne Jones taken at the crime scene, Adrianne's eyes half-lidded in death, gaping holes in her temple and cheek, her skull horribly crushed. Meyer thrust the photo in James's face. "How did you feel about her, James?" Meyer screamed.

James averted his gaze. "Feel about who?"

"Who, hell, asshole. This pretty thing right here. Don't look away, you son of a bitch."

"I . . . I didn't feel any way."

"Didn't feel any way? Didn't you love her?"

"I don't love anybody."

"Oh, yeah, you did. You loved her. You still love her? After you done this?"

"I didn't do anything," James said.

Meyer offered him the picture. "Take this, James."

The boy was stunned. "Huh?"

The detective scowled. "I said, take it."

Woodenly, James reached out and held the picture in his hands. His fingers trembled.

"Now, you loved her so much, you give her a big hug, you hear?" Meyer moved in closer. "I said, hug her, you asshole."

Tears streaming down his face, James pulled the photo to his bare chest. He gave Meyer a pleading look.

"You just hug the shit out of her, James." Meyer walked to the door, then turned back. "You just hug the shit out of her, and think about what you done to that girl." With that, Meyer left the cell and locked the door behind him, leaving James Drummond alone with one of the most gruesome sights imaginable.

Make no mistake that the foregoing is James Drummond's story, to date neither confirmed nor denied by the Grand Prairie Police Department.

As in all lawsuits there are two sides, and the plaintiff's assertions are likely exaggerated. Yet neither is it probable that the police held James for four days just to buddy around with the boy.

In any case, James Drummond stood up to four days of interrogation without confessing to a thing, and the detectives finally decided that they'd better make some sort of move. The forensics lab had gone over James's midnight blue Izusu pickup with fine-toothed combs and vacuum cleaners—eventually the crime-scene unit examined fifty-five items taken either from James's truck or his room at home—but found neither hairs, fibers, nor blood samples to place Adrianne Jones inside the vehicle at any time. As detectives grilled James behind closed doors, other cops wore down shoe leather questioning everyone who knew Adrianne or the suspect in the hope that someone could place them together on the night in question. No soap—other than Golden Chicken employees' recollection that Adrianne had hinted she was meeting James later that night, and Adrianne's brother's fuzzy memory of a pickup driving away in the dead of night, there was little or nothing to go on.

The detectives' choices at that point were to charge James officially with the murder or release him. Established procedure dictates that charges be filed or the suspect set free within forty-eight hours after an arrest, and Grand Prairie police had already exceeded the time limit. Normally they would have let James go and kept him under observation in hopes he would trip himself up, but this case was far from run-of-the-mill. Chief Harry Crum had already held a press conference and announced that his department had its man. Facing massive pressure to clear the case, detectives got their paperwork—such as it was—ready for the district attorney, and prepared to transport James from police headquarters to the county jail. Clay and Meyer handled the honors personally, loading the handcuffed suspect into the seat of an unmarked police vehicle and driving into town.

The Tarrant County Jail is in downtown Fort Worth on Belknap Street, a block from the ancient, domed, redbrick courthouse designated by the Texas Historical Society as one of the landmarks of the Lone Star State. The five-year-old Justice Center Building is across from the jail and one block down. Meyer and Clay drove down the ramp leading to the jail basement, turned James Drummond over to the county officials, then took their paperwork over to the Justice Center in search of an assistant district attorney willing to listen to them.

The official procedure for police seeking indictments in Tarrant County is first to contact the D.A.'s Intake Department. Intake, peopled with ADA's just out of law school, is theoretically the place where a decision is made to either accept or reject the case for prosecution based on the evidence in police files, but the fact is that Intake sees only cases of the open-and-shut variety. Veteran detectives understand that any case where the suspect wasn't caught with the smoking gun in his hand requires attention from a higher authority. Meyer and Clay bypassed Intake altogether and rode up to the tenth floor of the Justice Center. There they went from office to office in search of a prosecutor with time on his hands, and finally crowded into the cubbyhole of a veteran ADA named Curtis Stallings. As Stallings listened, the detectives sat down and pled their case. If they stood any chance at all of having James Drummond indicted, Meyer and Clay had some fast talking to do.

Just as veteran detectives understand that they should avoid taking certain files to the Intake Department, prosecutors who have been around the block a time or two know that policemen tend to be overzealous in rounding up suspects in cases that have received a lot of newspaper ink. Participants in the justice system often treat high-profile cases like people in a hot potato-tossing contest. If the cops can pass the case off to the district attorney's people, then the policemen's skirts are clean if the D.A. can't get a conviction.

But as long as there's no one under arrest, the heat stays on the police department.

Curtis Stallings listened noncommittally to detectives Meyer and Clay and, once they finished their presentation, agreed to keep the file and look into the matter. He knew about the murder of Adrianne Jones, of course, and had read in the paper that the Grand Prairie police had a suspect in custody. He also knew, however, that if the evidence against James Gregory Drummond was conclusive, the detectives would have stopped at Intake instead of coming to him. He told the policemen he'd get back to them regarding a possible indictment once he'd had time to go over the legal issues. The moment the door swung closed on Meyer and Clay, Curtis Stallings used the intercom to tell his boss that the D.A. was now in possession of the hot potato. Then he swiftly retreated to the law library.

Tall and broad, Curt Stallings has thick dark hair and wears a neatly trimmed beard. As a criminal prosecutor he's a bit of an oddity. Unlike most ADA's, he didn't graduate from law school with a burning desire to put the bad guys away. He spent his first few years after passing the bar in doing *pro bono* work in the Oriental community. Yet once he married a girl from Thailand and prepared to raise a family, he needed steadier employment. None of which means that Curtis Stallings doesn't take his job very seriously; he does, but he also has other interests. He's an aspiring novelist, and several teachers feel that if he could put his legal work aside for long enough to finish one of his partially completed books, a career as a professional writer could well be in store.

He spent a couple of days with the Adrianne Jones murder file in one hand and a lawbook in the other. Deciding whether or not to prosecute a criminal case is a simpler process than most laypersons would think. Contrary to the public presumption-of-innocence concept, the advantage in a trial hardly ever lies with defense attorneys. Judges take pains in explaining to jurors that the person on trial is innocent until the state proves otherwise, but juror mentality works exactly the opposite. Members of jury pools usually feel that if the guy hadn't done something wrong, the state wouldn't have him on trial in the first place. ADA's understand this, and know that if they can get the case before a jury, the battle is ninety percent won.

So the decision process amounts to determining if the jury will ever have a chance to deliberate. Juries decide matters of fact—whether the accused on trial really committed the crime, in other words—but interpretation of the law is up to the judge. The law in criminal trials is pretty clear. The burden is on the state to produce enough evidence to allow the jury to make a decision, and if the state fails to meet this burden, the judge is required to give an instructed verdict of acquittal.

The case against James Gregory Drummond was incredibly weak. There wasn't a single witness to put him in Adrianne Jones's company on the night of the murder; nor had anything turned up in the forensics lab's examination of James's pickup to place Adrianne in the passenger seat at any time. Despite ransacking James's possessions, police had failed to come up with a murder weapon. GPPD, in fact, had exactly what they had started with—James's vagueness over his whereabouts on the night of the murder coupled with Adrianne's brother's recollection of a pickup driving away from the house, none of which, barring corroborating evidence, was likely to be admissible. What Stallings saw was a case that, if it went to trial, was certain to result in an instructed verdict, and after two days of research he called the detectives and told them so.

The Grand Prairie cops' reaction to the ADA's decision was less than cordial. They had a front-burner murder investigation going, where their chief had gone out on a limb and announced that his men had cracked the case, and to back off now would cause the department great embarrassment. Meyer and Clay put their heads together, then huddled with the brass upstairs. The decision was unanimous. If the district attorney of

Tarrant County, Texas, didn't want to undertake aggressive prosecution against James Gregory Drummond, then someone was going to raise hell.

That someone turned out to be Chief Harry Crum. The dapper Grand Prairie law enforcement head drove down to the district attorney's office and demanded a conference. Crum met with Curtis Stallings behind closed doors for over an hour, explaining in no uncertain terms the consequences of a refusal to prosecute. Curtis Stallings held his ground—they just didn't have a case against this guy. If the GPPD could come up with the slightest thread of prosecutable evidence, then the Tarrant County D.A. would go forth with both guns blazing. But if the district attorney went into court with *this* ammunition, then Drummond would walk, and through double jeopardy would be immune from prosecution if the cops should build a case in the future.

Chief Crum asserted that his department didn't have time to wait. He had made a commitment, and if Stallings didn't offer any satisfaction, then Crum was going over the ADA's head. Fine, Stallings said, picking up his file, I'll go with you. And that's what they did, taking the case down the hall to the D.A.'s first assistant Allan Levy. Levy, as the police chief already knew, had a tendency to look at things from a different perspective.

* * *

Ask an elected district attorney the specifics of any case under his supervision, and the D.A. will tell you with a smile that he will have to get back to you. Then he'll ask his first assistant what is going on. The first assistant runs the department while the D.A. concerns himself with political matters.

Tim Curry, the district attorney of Tarrant County, has been elected for several consecutive terms. Allan Levy was around before Curry took the office and knows the ropes, and while he privately agreed with Curtis Stallings that the case against James Drummond was weak, it was his duty to keep from ruffling any feathers between the D.A. and the various police departments in the county. It fell on Allan Levy to find another direction in which to toss the hot potato. And as any good first assistant knows, the grand jury is always there as backup.

The grand jury process is, of course, closed to the public. Grand jurors meet in secret, with the district attorney's representative as their only outside counsel, and consider cases that the D.A.'s office wants to pursue for indictment purposes. The grand jury may either return a true bill (an indictment) or a no-bill, which amounts to a decision that the D.A. doesn't have enough evidence to move forward with the case.

At least that is the theory. In practice, however,

the grand jury works quite differently. Grand jury members aren't lawyers and so depend almost entirely on the D.A.'s representative to tell them what to do. If the district attorney tells them to indict, grand jurors comply. Occasionally, when there is pressure on the district attorney to move forward with a case that the D.A. knows is weak, the D.A. may present the case to the grand jurors in such a manner as to prompt a no-bill.

Whatever his intent as to the final outcome, Levy presented the case to the grand jury just after New Year's Day, and announced to the press that it might take weeks for grand jurors to reach a conclusion. In the meantime James Drummond would remain in jail.

His parents had retained a lawyer, Richard Price, who decided it was time to take the bull by the horns. He approached Levy with an interesting idea. Why not, asked Price, have the boy take a lie-detector test?

Levy was stunned. "You mean the Grand Prairie police didn't give him one?"

Price shook his head.

"Well, I guess we'd better call our polygraph man," he said.

On January 5, 1996, guards brought James Drummond from the jail and took him into a special room. There they sat him in a chair, tightened a rubber strap around his chest to monitor his breathing, and attached pulse-count readers to both of his arms. The polygraph examiner was ready across the table.

The test consumed a couple of hours, and around mid-afternoon the examiner brought the results over to the Justice Center and left them with Allan Levy. He read over the polygraph examiner's findings, then picked up his phone, dialed the Grand Prairie police, and asked for Detective Dennis Clay. When Clay came on the line, Levy was brief and to the point. "You're back to square one," Levy said. "It seems you've arrested the wrong guy."

Aside from the obvious trauma to the Drummond family, the time wasted in charging James with Adrianne Jones's murder left the real killers' trail extremely cold. Once James Drummond, blinking into lenses of television cameras, emerged from the jail on January 7 and went home with his mother and father, detectives found themselves with no more leads than they'd had on the day Gary Foster found Adrianne's body in his field.

There is a resultant hangover with police once their main suspect is cleared in any crime. Although detectives are reluctant to admit it, there is always a feeling that they had their man all along, but the criminal has somehow defeated the justice system. After James Drummond's release, the investigation into Adrianne's murder came to a virtual standstill. The file remained open, of course, but from that time on, detectives responded to questions from reporters or Adrianne's mother with a series of we're-working-on-it's, if indeed they responded at all. There's nothing in the file today to indicate that Clay and Meyer did another thing until they received the call out of the blue from Annapolis, Maryland.

During December, as James Drummond sat alone in his cell at the Tarrant County Jail, David Graham took his father's credit card and went on another shopping spree. He bought new coats, both for Diane and her mother, and also picked up a few CD's for himself. He spent Christmas Eve at the Zamoras' house in South Fort Worth, where a good time was had by all.

# 10

Newspaper and magazine stories lead one to believe that Diane kept her silence for many months, then opened up to near-total strangers long after she and David had gotten away with murder. Such a scenario would be as stunning as the crime itself, because Diane and David were kids with no prior criminal records, yet they're given credit for showing an outward veneer of normalcy that would be the envy of hardened convicts. The fact is that the lovers' silence is only a myth. David and Diane did tell others about the murder. A number of others.

Police and prosecutors have leaked to the press that David told a Civil Air Patrol friend of his named Clayton Willis while the two of them were out drinking just a few days after the crime, and described the murder in graphic detail. Clayton Willis is in the service now, having enlisted just after graduation from high school, and may or may not appear at trial as a subpoenaed witness. Willis is staunchly loyal to David. Therefore, the things he might say on the witness stand make prosecutors nervous, and it's an unwritten rule among lawyers that one never puts on a witness without knowing the witness's testimony in advance. There is also an unconfirmed rumor that David confided in B. C. Horne, the boy whose home Diane and David visited to clean themselves up after murdering Adrianne. B.C., when questioned by a reporter about his knowledge of the crime, drew up at attention and responded with, "No comment, sir."

David wasn't the only one who talked. Diane confessed to a girl who lived down the street from her, Sandra Trevino, who was also her classmate at Crowley High. Ever since the case broke in the newspapers, Sandra has been in hiding. Her mother has shielded her from the press, and she's apparently living in another town.

What is surprising isn't that Diane and David kept their silence, but that they weren't apprehended within weeks. The fact that all these youngsters kept their knowledge of a grisly homicide hidden from police is a comment on the overall effectiveness of the investigation, and also a comment on the values held by the teenagers themselves. Concealment of knowledge of a crime isn't a jailable offense in Texas—though in many other states it is—so David and Diane's confidants will answer only to themselves. In a few years they may look back and wonder what they were thinking.

Diane has told another story which, if true, identifies confidants who don't have youthful inexperience as an excuse for keeping quiet. According to her, just a few days after the murder she sat down one night at supper and told her mother and father. Neither Carlos nor Gloria Zamora will comment one way or the other, but Diane says that her parents listened in horror as she told the grisly story, then immediately telephoned El Templo de Juan and had a conference with Diane's grandfather. Miguel Mendoza then came to the house, where Diane repeated her story to him.

Two days later, Miguel Mendoza called the entire family together at El Templo and delivered a sermon in Spanish during which he outlined his granddaughter's sins to one and all. The clan then joined in a prayer session, after which Miguel Mendoza told Diane that the murder was something she'd done in a previous life, and that she had a brand-new existence from that day forward.

Though Diane has told this story more than once, some of her aunts and uncles have said that the incident never happened. Carlos and Gloria appeared before the grand jury hearing the case, and stated under oath that they had no knowledge of the murder before Diane's arrest.

Even if the story is true, it isn't all that shocking that Carlos and Gloria wouldn't turn in their own daughter—any parent would be torn under the circumstances—but that the entire family would know and then keep the murder under their hats is very odd. Equally unbelievable is the fact that Diane and David could be so loose with their secret and, nine months after the murder, still be free as birds on the wing.

Regardless of what they told others in private, Diane and David went through the spring semester of their senior years in high school doing all the senior things. They attended two dances—the junior-senior proms held at both Crowley and Mansfield Highs—and the ROTC banquet at Mansfield, where because of David's position as commandant, they shared the head table with the high school principal and members of the faculty. David went to both proms decked out in a tuxedo; Diane wore a white off-shoulder formal to one and a blue floor-length evening dress to the other. David bought both of Diane's outfits on his father's credit card.

During the Crowley Jr.-Sr. Prom, Alton Ruiz noticed Diane standing alone near a giant punch bowl and asked her to dance. She agreed, and the couple took a spin across the floor. In the middle of the number, David appeared from nowhere, tapped Alton on the shoulder, and said he was cutting in. Alton nodded in disappointment and started to walk away.

Diane was suddenly short with David. "The song isn't over. Can't you wait? Come on, Alton, let's finish." She extended both arms in Alton's direction.

David's features twisted in anger. "Don't forget our secret, Diane. You just don't forget it, you hear me?" With that, David spun on his heel and stalked away, leaving Diane and Alton Ruiz staring at each other.

"What was that all about?" Alton finally said.

"Nothing," said Diane. "He was just talking is all."

David easily snared one of the Civil Air Patrol's Air Force Academy appointments that spring and, with a personal recommendation from Vice President Al Gore to add to his application, received his acceptance from academy officials in early March. Although his high school grades weren't up to par, David was one of those fortunate youngsters who test well. His PSAT scores were in the lower thirteen hundreds, giving him honorable mention in the National Merit Scholar competition, so his standing in his class was never an issue with the service school.

Diane's acceptance to the Naval Academy was more of a struggle. Air Force, where she really wanted to go in order to be with David through college, turned her down flat, and her high school grades and SAT scores placed her on the bubble where Annapolis was concerned. Of the twelve hundred appointments handed out that spring, two hundred were reserved for females per federal decree. Additionally, applications from minorities received preferential consideration. Even so, when Diane drove over to Dallas for a personal interview with a Naval Academy representative in early April, she was by no means a shoo-in for acceptance. She impressed in her interview—the Naval Academy rep, who is also a Dallas banker, remembers very well that she was the only applicant with whom he spoke who came unaccompanied by parents—and, in part on the strength of a personal appeal by Fort Worth Congressman Pete Geren, she was accepted.

Diane quickly became the toast of the Hispanic community once the word got around. *La Estrella*, the Spanish language supplement to the *Ft. Worth Star-Telegram*, called requesting an interview, and when the newspaper learned that Diane's fiancé was to be an Air Force cadet, it decided to feature the dream couple in a front-page spread. David and Diane were all smiles for the interview, conducted at Jerry Graham's house in Mansfield, and announced their wedding date as August 13, 2000, a week after their projected graduations. Diane told the reporter that she planned to join the Air Force when she finished the Naval Academy—it's a little-known fact that academy graduates can fulfill their military obligations in different branches of the service from the school they attended—so that she and David could spend their careers together. The photo accompanying the article shows Diane and David packing for their respective trips to Maryland and Colorado, and in the picture both are grinning ear to ear.

Two days after the interview, Diane drove David to DFW Airport to catch his plane for Colorado Springs, kissed him good-bye at the gate, and stood at the window as the jet taxied out to the runway. Three days after that, Carlos and Gloria waved to Diane through the same window as her own plane departed for Annapolis. So the lovers parted temporarily, secure in the belief that their futures were bright, and that any problems they might have had in Texas were far behind them.

# 11

*Annapolis, Maryland*

Plebe Summer at the United States Naval Academy is a grueling trial, whether measured by thermometer, humidity gauge, stress test, or any standard known to man. For a hundred and fifty-one Julys a few good men—or in more recent years, a few good persons—have competed fiercely for their appointments to the Academy, then shortly after their arrival at this sauna on the Chesapeake have questioned their sanity for doing so. Before fall classes get underway, first-year students are subjected to seven weeks of hell.

Their introduction to the Academy is pleasant enough. Most newcomers fly into Baltimore-Washington Airport, where upperclassmen in starch-pressed uniforms greet them with smiles, herd them into buses, and entertain them on the short ride to the campus with a flow of tour-guide dialogue. The buses enter the grounds through Gate Number Eight, the main and most scenic approach, where Marine guards wave them past the eight-foot barrier into an expanse of clipped lawns and majestic shade trees. Halsey Field House—formerly the Middies' basketball arena—is a mammoth hulk on the horizon, and the road ahead leads directly toward the heat-slick Chesapeake River. The buildings are imposing granite, sporting copper roofs green with age. What appears to be many structures is really only a single edifice; Bancroft Hall, the Academy's lone dormitory, houses the entire student body and consists of countless wings connected by a series of ground-floor corridors. The buses halt near the main entry, where plebes receive room and company assignments. Their first night aboard they go on liberty and casually stroll the avenues of Annapolis proper. It's their final taste of freedom until Plebe Summer ends. The following dawn marks Inauguration Day.

Many parents attend I-Day, and with moms and dads keeping watchful eyes, the stripers—upperclassmen, so-called because of the gilt lines on their uniform shoulder boards—hold the harassment down to a minimum. Reveille sounds at 0500 hours, at which time the stripers spend the morning issuing dress whites to the plebes and teaching them to salute. Male recruits have their heads shaved while the women's hair is clipped above the collar line. Thus presentable, the plebes assemble, with parents and naval brass looking on, for a public swearing-in. It's an impressive sight, a thousand young men and women, right hands raised, repeating the oath as fighter jets lay smoke trails overhead. After the ceremony, plebes have a few moments to say good-byes to parents and siblings. Then all civilians are escorted from the grounds, and the plebes enter Bancroft Hall. From that moment on, they're at their superiors' mercy.

"Maggot!" or "Dirtbag!" are the more pleasant terms that stripers use in in-your-face confrontations, though with company officers safely out of earshot, the insults reach a more basic level. Shoes show mandatory spitshines; if the gleam isn't perfect, the mash of a striper's heel pulverizes the entire effect and the plebe must repolish his or her footwear from scratch. Beds must be quarter-bounce tight, clothing aligned in lockers with hangers an inch apart and creases precisely parallel. Plebes dress exactly alike, in white jumpers over shorts and T-shirts with Dixie Cups—that's the official name—perched just so on their heads.

Rooms in Bancroft Hall do have showers, though the toilets are in the heads down the corridor, but bathing creates more nightmares for the plebes. If the striper's white-gloved finger shows the slightest residue when rubbed on shower tiles, the plebes are in for it. Quarters inspections are daily, sometimes hourly, and without prior notice. Since the routine doesn't leave enough time to clean the showers, spit-shine the shoes, and arrange the lockers every day, plebes learn to improvise. They go for days on end without bathing and sleep on the floor so as not to disturb the perfectly made beds. Stripers are former plebes, of course, so are on to all the shortcuts, and often burst into the room in the middle of the night to discipline the floor sleepers.

Daily routines for plebes are always the same. Reveille blasts recruits awake at 0500 hours, after which plebes have fifteen minutes to assemble on the parade ground for an hour of physical training: side-straddle hops, push-ups, sit-ups, laps around the field. Then, just as they are ready to drop from exhaustion, breakfast is served.

There is only one dining room on campus, King's Hall, located in the basement at Bancroft, and meals are torture. Plebes must sit at attention, backs ramrod straight, fannies on the front edges of their chairs, while stripers roam the aisles and scream insults at the tops of their lungs. There's even a rigid order in which plebes must eat. Fork spears food, rises straight up from the plate to lip level, then deposits food into mouth on a line parallel to the table. Plebes must eat every bite or pay the consequences. After breakfast are marching drills, classes, more physical training, more classes—overseen by leather-lunged stripers—all day long and into the night until taps blow at ten hundred hours. Plebes' nights are restless in spite of their exhaustion. They start awake and sit bolt upright at intervals, frightened that they have slept through reveille, then realize it's the middle of the night, roll over, and toss and turn.

Diane Zamora, had she known what she was getting into, might never have boarded the plane from Dallas. Nothing she'd learned in Civil Air Patrol meetings had prepared her for this. She'd never been a very good trooper to begin with; in CAP she'd always found someone—David for the past half year, other friends before that—to sympathize with her over her foul-ups. But at the Naval Academy other plebes were too busy with their own problems to worry about Diane and—in her eyes, anyway—treated her as inferior. Here when she tripped over her own feet in marching drills, one of the stripers was in her face immediately. Physical training was more agony than she'd ever experienced in cross-country running at Crowley High.

She was drained, discouraged, more exhausted than she'd ever been in her life, and cried herself to sleep every night after taps. She had a computer in her room—a mandatory purchase at service academies, with the sale price deducted in increments from her pay each month—and could communicate with David every day by e-mail, but his messages on her monitor screen were no substitute for being with him. As the days expanded into weeks and Diane grew more and more insecure, she began to search desperately for some way to force those around her to treat her as an equal, and to make her own feelings of inadequacy disappear.

### Colorado Springs, Colorado

Three-fourths of a continent to the west, David Graham was well within his element. While the Air Force Academy Doolies' induction routine is every bit as grueling as the Annapolis Plebes', it's more bearable because of the weather. Doolies sleep under blankets with open windows, wake up every morning in fifty-degree weather, and perform their calisthenics with snow-capped Rocky Mountain peaks as a backdrop, inhaling thin, cool air as they briskly run the obstacle course.

David was in good shape to begin with, and grew physically stronger every day. Whereas the rigors of Naval Academy life were wearing Diane to a frazzle, David took everything the Air Force could dish out and thrived on it. Upperclassmen screaming insults in his ear didn't seem to bother him; he accepted every order with a cheery "Yes, sir!" He quickly became a platoon leader, then a squadron leader, and the officers in charge of his unit began to use the young man from Texas and his enthusiasm as an example to other Doolies.

During nightly gripe sessions at the dormitory, David would climb all over other cadets about their complaining, telling them either to get with the program or resign from the Air Force.

David didn't even offer Diane any sympathy. He seemed embarrassed by his Naval Academy sweetheart's nightly e-mail messages, and often read Diane's Internet grumblings aloud to his roommate. He began to tweak Diane, chiding her through cyberspace about being such a crybaby. She responded angrily, typing terse messages to the effect that he was heartless and uncaring. Just before signing off one evening, she put a single sentence on David's monitor: Don't forget our secret, David. If there was a veiled threat within the message, David didn't catch on.

Early in August, he pulled a boner that may forever come back to haunt him. He sent Diane a couple of messages regarding a female cadet whom he identified as "Sandy." (Apparently he made this person up, because there are no Sandys in the 1996–97 freshman class enrolled at the Air Force Academy; there are three Sandras, but all were in different squadrons and didn't even know David.) According to what he told Diane, Sandy had the hots for him. He further wrote that he was doing all he could not to succumb to Sandy's advances, but didn't know how long he could resist. Whether Sandy was real or imagined, David's motive in throwing her up to Diane is pretty transparent; he was trying to make her jealous. Considering Diane's state of mind, however, pulling her chain over another female seems like a very poor idea.

### Annapolis

Jay Guild arrived from Chicago with a pretty good idea what he was getting into, and wasn't particularly worried. Tall and slim, Jay was a tough kid and figured that Plebe Summer wasn't any worse than Navy boot camp for enlisted men. Since he was going to be in the service one way or the other, he knew that Navy life as an officer was far better than what was in store for deck hands. Though not gung-ho like David Graham, Jay made a better-than-average plebe. He took the harassment with a stiff upper lip, never complained, and went about his business with the attitude that, what the hell, two freaking months, a guy can live with anything.

He noticed the petite Hispanic girl from Texas early on. He couldn't help but notice her, in fact. In marching she was always out of step, in laps around the field she finished last every time, and she dragged herself through the day like a zombie. Jay felt sorry for her at first, and went out of his way to try to offer her pick-me-ups in the way of encouragement, but she responded to his friendliness with a series of vacant stares. He decided that she was one of these my-own-demons-to-fight kind of people, and after a couple of attempts to get to know her, he pretty much left her alone.

About three weeks into the Plebe Summer ordeal, Diane took the initiative and approached Jay. The move surprised him, the pretty fellow plebe who'd rebuffed his attempts at friendliness before, now sidling up to him in the evenings before reveille, or showing up at the door to his dorm room and shooting the bull. Jay supposes he was somewhat attracted to her, though looking back on it he really isn't certain. Since she stated clearly that she was engaged to a cadet at the Air Force Academy, he had no inkling that they were to be anything other than friends.

Her relationship with Jay couldn't have gone beyond the point of friendship during Plebe Summer, even if the couple had been panting for each other. Plebes can't go on liberty, are watched by upperclassmen at all times, and are generally too whipped for romantic dalliances at the end of the day. In addition, the rules forbid dating for a midshipman's entire freshman year.

Once Diane warmed up to Jay, she began to talk his ear off. Jay soon felt as well acquainted with David Graham as he was with his high school buddies back in Illinois. Every day Diane would give Jay a blow-by-blow of what she and David had transmitted through the Internet, and very shortly Jay was as familiar with everything the couple had done together back in Texas—well, not *everything*—as he would have been if he'd been there in person. He knew Diane's parents' names as well as those of all her siblings. As the summer rolled by, Jay became certain that Diane was madly in love with her Air Force fiancé.

### Colorado Springs

As platonic as her relationship with Jay Guild was, Diane painted for David a completely different picture. After David's initial e-mail outlining his potential thing with "Sandy," he didn't hear a word from Diane for three solid days. His attempt at making her jealous having backfired, David panicked and sent her several urgent messages. Still he got no reply. Diane's failure to respond worried him to death; he kept his roommate awake until all hours, fooling with his computer, checking his e-mail, pacing the floor.

Finally, on the fourth night, Diane got in touch. She typed out two terse sentences: I have a boyfriend here, David. His name is Jay. Then she clicked offline. David stared at his monitor for a long time. Then he spent the rest of the night furiously typing the same messages over and over: Where are you, Diane? Talk to me. Talk to me. Diane rejected her e-mail, however.

David wasn't through. The next day he fired off a letter to Annapolis authorities to the effect that a midshipman named Jay was sexually harassing

Diane. He even composed a nasty e-mail for Jay; he had to delete the message after learning that without a last name he had no way to send the thing. Frantic, David charged around the dorm at night, telling everyone what he'd do to Jay if he ever got his hands on him. His roommate, growing sick of it all, put in a request for a change of quarters. One thing was for certain. Whatever David's motives in telling Diane about another woman in his life, she'd certainly turned the tables but good.

### *Annapolis*

By mid-August, Plebe Summer was almost over. The fall term would begin in a week. While a plebe's life is no bed of roses even when classes are in session, the stripers then have their plates full with schoolwork of their own, and therefore less time in which to make things miserable for the plebes.

Diane showed up at Jay Guild's door one night about an hour before taps with things on her mind. She sat down at his computer desk as he reclined on his bed. Finally she announced, "David and I have broken up."

He was surprised. It was the first indication he'd had that Diane and her fiancé were having problems. He said, "Kind of sudden, isn't it?"

"Things have been building up," she said. "He's been seeing this girl out there."

Jay's eyebrows lifted. "Just like that?"

Diane seemed thoughtful but angry. "He's making a mistake, messing with me."

"You're just mad," Jay said. "Give yourself time to think things out."

Diane began to sniffle. "We were supposed to get married. If I hadn't thought we were, we never would have done this awful thing."

It wasn't the first time Diane had referred to the secret she had with David, but Jay wasn't the nosy type and hadn't pressed her on the issue. He didn't do so now. "Things will work out," he said.

"Oh, no they won't. Not this time. And after what I saw him do . . ."

Jay tried to joke her out of it. "It couldn't be all that bad."

"Oh, yes, it could. David killed this girl, you know."

Jay was stunned. "Oh, come on."

Diane was emphatic. "Oh, yes, he did. It was a girl he'd been messing around with. He told me he had been, and told me he'd kill her to show he really loved me. He said he was going to, and I saw him do it."

Jay's laugh was nervous and just a bit frightened. "You're just putting me on."

Diane assumed an odd vacant look. "He killed her, Jay."

"Well, if he did," Jay said. "I don't want to

know about it. I don't want to hear about it, Diane."

She tearfully regarded her lap for a moment, then looked back up. "He killed her, Jay."

Jay Guild says today that he'd give anything if Diane had never told him about the murder, and also that once she did, he wishes he'd turned her in the very next day. But the truth was that he thought she was pulling his chain. In a situation like Plebe Summer, it was pretty common for them to sit around the dorm at night swapping lies. As the hours dragged on, the stories grew wilder and wilder. So, though no one had told him before that they'd witnessed a murder, Jay filed Diane's tale away with the rest of the lies he'd heard. As time went by, however, he went from a feeling of not believing her at all to one of not being sure.

Once she'd opened up to Jay, Diane brought the subject up just about every time they were together—in the line before chow, nights around the dorm, and, once the fall term began, during the two Saturday liberties they spent together. She never gave him all the details—he never asked for them—but her story was always the same. David Graham had been unfaithful to Diane with another girl back in Texas, had told Diane about the transgression in a moment of remorse, then had offered to kill the other girl as an act of penance. Diane had then witnessed the killing in person.

It's significant that since Diane's first revelations of the crime at Annapolis, the story has changed somewhat. She originally told Jay that the murder had been David's idea, and gave the impression that she had been a passive witness to the crime. In David's confession, however—and in Diane's, given just a day later—both stated that they had jointly planned the killing and had carried it out together.

Jay Guild was uncomfortable hearing about the murder, but other than changing the subject whenever Diane brought it up, he never really discussed it with her. When asked after the story broke in the media, he said that he had never reported Diane because he didn't believe her, and also because the two had become so close that he felt almost as if she were part of his family. Jay Guild, like other friends in whom Diane and David had confided back in Texas, never revealed Diane's story to anyone else until after the confessions. In opening up to Jay, however, Diane was setting the stage for events that finally would bring the investigation into the murder of Adrianne Jones to an end.

Carlos and Gloria Zamora made the sixteen-hundred mile drive from Fort Worth to Annapolis and visited Diane during the week after classes began. She was tickled to death to learn that she was still the pride of the Hispanic community back home, and her parents brought her greetings from all of her aunts, uncles, and cousins.

Like any pair of parent-tourists, the Zamoras became camera bugs on the trip. They photographed Diane all over the campus, their daughter smiling, laughing, saluting, posing before statues and on the bank of the Chesapeake River. Once they handed their camera to a student and had their picture taken together, with Diane standing between her parents with her arms around their waists.

Diane tugged Jay Guild over and introduced him to Carlos and Gloria as her "new boyfriend," which caused them to exchange astonished glances. Actually, they both felt a sense of relief. They hadn't been that crazy about David to begin with. Carlos then asked Jay if he'd pose with Diane, and Jay obliged. Carlos took the picture with a mounted cannon as a backdrop, and with Jay and Diane saluting in rigid posture. Diane's bearing in the finished photo is perfect with one exception. The proper way to deliver a military salute is from the position of attention, with right-hand fingers straight and barely touching the hatband, and with the left-hand fingers curled alongside the pant leg. While Diane is in perfect position for the salute, the fingers of her left hand jut straight out in an awkward manner, and this is as close as Diane Zamora can come to making a fist to this very day.

Bickering among roommates, particularly females, has been common since our first college opened its doors; in fact, there are more roommates who don't get along than those who do. Campus officials have learned over the years that it's easier to establish a liberal change-of-quarters policy than to put up with the complaining. The United States Naval Academy is no different in this regard, and plebes live three to a room, so it's easier for a pair to gang up on the odd roomie out.

Diane went through three sets of roomies during her two months at Annapolis. Her first switch of quarters came after only a week, at her request, and the reason for the change isn't known. Her second set of roommates lasted a month and a half. Both of these girls complained to officials that Diane's moaning over the conditions of Plebe Summer kept them awake at night and that she refused to do her part in housekeeping chores. Both requested that they be moved together or Diane be moved alone. In other words, it was her or them. In view of subsequent events, there is a strong possibility that her roommates had a different motive, but their move requests listed only a lack of compatibility. One being easier to relocate than two, Diane received orders to pack her belongings.

\* \* \*

Jenifer McKearney and Mandy Gotch had had roommate problems that were far different from any of the other young women in Bancroft Hall. They'd gotten along pretty well with their roomie. None of the three had put in a move request or had any intention of doing so. But one morning in late August, Mandy and Jenifer woke up with their roommate dead.

The findings of the coroner were that the deceased young woman committed suicide. Navy officials won't comment on what she took before going to bed, but there are illegal drugs at the Academy just as on most college campuses in America. Plebe Summer affects its victims in different ways. Whatever emotional toll that the death of the roommate took on Mandy and Jenifer, they had more stress in store for them. Within a few days after Academy personnel rolled the body out the door, Diane Zamora came in, hauling her luggage behind her.

As Diane unpacked her belongings, Jenifer and Mandy exchanged looks that included a lot of rolling of their eyes. They knew Diane, both in person and by reputation around the campus, and a inveterate complainer was something they didn't need. Plus there were other rumors floating about concerning Diane.

\* \* \*

*Close-up*

This young woman has asked that her name be withheld. "It can cause me major grief," she says.

"You mean, from the Academy?" the interviewer asks.

"Among others."

"That would be a restriction of your right to speak out."

"There's nothing official. There's this pact, sort of, just not to talk about it."

"Then why are you?"

She watches the interviewer with clear gray eyes. "I think I'd like to get the record straight, about some things that went on."

"Then we've got a common goal," the interviewer says. "So it's your feeling," he continues, "that more than just a few people around the Academy knew about Diane."

She shrugs. "I knew her and then I didn't know her. I hadn't been up there but a couple of weeks when this girl points her out and says, 'Look out for that chick there. She's really weird, and claims she and a guy killed this girl one time.'"

"Hmm. Did you ever hear Diane say anything like that?"

"Not me. I kept a million miles away from her. The way she acted was scary."

"Why do you think, with a secret like that, she'd go around telling people."

"Because she thought it sounded tough."

"Not that she was only scared and homesick?" the interviewer says.

"I know she had her roommates scared to death, the way she talked at night."

"You mean, Jenifer Kearney and . . ." The interviewer checks his notepad. "Mandy—"

"Not them, the girls before. Jenifer and Mandy were scared before she ever moved in with them. Their other roommate died."

"I know that. And there's this thing about the boy they kicked out of school."

She nods for emphasis. "Jay Guild. Only, he resigned."

"Officially he resigned. He says he did so before they kicked him out."

"That's one reason I wanted to talk to you," she says. "They talk about their honor code, but there were a lot of plebes up there talking about her and what she claimed she did."

"Then why," the interviewer says, "do you think they'd single out one student, Jay Guild, for punishment?"

She smirks. "That doesn't take any genius to figure out. This is the Navy, mister. They singled him out because he was the only one with his name in the paper. It's what I wanted to set the record straight on. A lot of midshipmen knew about it. Jay Guild got royally screwed, if you want my opinion."

* * *

There can be little doubt at this point that Jay Guild wasn't the only member of the plebe class with whom Diane had discussed the murder of Adrianne Jones. There was simply too much talk, and Jay Guild swears that he never discussed what Diane told him with anyone. But by the time Diane moved into her third room at the Academy, both Mandy and Jenifer had heard that Diane had been bragging about a killing back in Texas and that, as a result, many of the female plebes were frightened to death of her.

Diane barely had time to stow her gear in her locker and place David's picture on top before taps sounded. She'd barely spoken to Mandy and Jenifer as she unpacked, and the three roommates were all in bed when they started their first conversation together.

After a few minutes of small talk, Jenifer pointed at the framed photo on top of Diane's locker. "Is that your boyfriend?"

"We've been engaged, but now I don't know," Diane said.

Mandy asked, "What, you're not going together anymore?"

"We'll always be together, somehow," Diane said. "We've got something binding us together."

Mandy and Jenifer exchanged a look. This conversation was right in line with what they'd heard, but it was hard for them to believe that Diane was so open about it.

Finally Jenifer said, "What did the two of you do, kill somebody?"

There were long seconds of silence, broken only by the soft breathing of the three young women in their beds.

Finally Diane said, so faintly that the other girls could barely hear, "Yes. Killed somebody. That's exactly what we did."

Just why Diane chose to speak out while she was at the Naval Academy is purely speculation, but a few guesses can be safely hazarded. For one thing, Diane was terribly inexperienced, and the trip to Maryland was the first time she'd been farther from Fort Worth than Mineral Wells (about sixty miles). That word could get from Annapolis, Maryland, all the way back to Fort Worth, Texas, probably never occurred to her.

Second—and most significantly—the people to whom she was telling these stories were her peers. She didn't consider the other plebes a threat to her. After all, the kids she'd confided in back in Fort Worth had kept quiet about the murder, so why wouldn't these plebes do so as well?

Finally, Diane was completely out of her element, and she felt terribly inferior. Telling about the murder had a certain shock value and, for a short time anyway, made her stand out in the other students' eyes.

Nine long months after Adrianne's murder, though, Diane Zamora had finally misjudged her audience.

Plebe Summer at Annapolis is the college chaplain's busiest time of the year. A thousand kids, most of whom have never been away from home, subjected to a rigorous schedule and never ending insults hurled by stripers, find the chaplain's to be the nearest available shoulder on which to cry. Many take advantage of the chaplain's comfort on a daily basis. So, on the morning of August 28, 1996, when Jenifer McKearney and Mandy Gotch came in for a talk, the chaplain assumed he was in for more of the same. He was wrong, however, and the tale these young women had to tell left the chaplain in a quandary as to how to proceed.

# 12

The chaplain is the only one in the Navy immune to the chain of command, and he bypassed channels, taking the story directly to the commandant of the Naval Academy. The Academy has suffered a number of embarrassments of late, including a drug ring uncovered on campus and nine midshipmen implicated in an interstate car-theft ring, but a student's possible involvement in a homicide was by far the worst. The Navy had to proceed very carefully. The female plebes' story sounded preposterous, but the charges were too serious to ignore. At the same time, the Academy wasn't about to issue charges against Diane Zamora or anyone else without first being sure what they had. The commandant first swore the chaplain to secrecy, then called in his legal adviser, Lieutenant Commander Patrick McCarthy. The three huddled behind closed doors, then McCarthy returned to his office and got on the phone.

Interestingly, Diane was finished at the Naval Academy even if her story turned out to be pure fantasy. By now she'd become too much of a disrupting factor on campus for the Navy to keep her on board. If McCarthy had failed to turn up a single homicide in the state of Texas that matched her story, Diane would have received her walking papers anyway. As things turned out, McCarthy almost didn't find what he was looking for.

He first called the Fort Worth and Crowley police departments and asked if these cities had any unsolved murders on the books to match what Diane had told her roommates, but neither department had any record of such a crime. McCarthy reported the results of his contacts to the commandant.

The matter could have ended right then and there if Diane hadn't implicated David Graham. If Diane's hometown police had nothing on record, the Naval officers reasoned, then what about the Air Force Academy kid? They didn't even know David's name at the time, much less where he was from, but had enough fragments of the story from the female plebes to believe that Diane's boyfriend was from a neighboring community to hers. So try them all, the commandant ordered, every town within a fifty-mile radius. It was a tall order, but McCarthy went back to work, using a map of north-central Texas he found in a highway guide.

McCarthy doesn't remember how many phone calls he made during the next twenty-four hours, but there were enough to make his button-pushing finger sore. Because of their out-of-the-way positions on the Texas map, he almost bypassed Mansfield and Grand Prairie altogether. In fact, he never did contact the Grand Prairie police, but just as he was ready to give up in frustration, he finally ran his finger along Road 1187 on the map, from Crowley through Rendon and Bloodworth. More as an afterthought than anything else, McCarthy put in a call to the Mansfield P.D. He made the connection around one in the afternoon on Thursday, August 29. Steve Noonkester was on duty that day, and as luck would have it, he picked up the phone in person.

Noonkester didn't waste time with the telephone, but drove around the lake and showed up at Grand Prairie police headquarters around two o'clock. He went straight to Deputy Chief Geary's office. Geary rang up detectives Meyer and Clay, who, nine months after James Drummond's botched arrest, no longer had the Adrianne Jones murder as a front-burner item. The four men had a lengthy meeting behind closed doors.

The policemen were skeptical at first. Since Adrianne's murder they'd received countless leads similar to this one. Yet two calls, one to Crowley High School and another to the

Mansfield newspaper, identified Diane Zamora's fiancé as David Christopher Graham. David's involvement made this trip more promising than most, if for no other reason than Linda Jones's description of a call to Adrianne from "David in cross-country." They contacted Mansfield High to learn that David had indeed been a member of the cross-country team while a student there. Detective Clay had a vague recollection of interviewing David at the high school, but didn't remember what the boy looked like. So while the policemen agreed that this was probably another red herring, they decided to follow up on the Naval Academy's call.

Early Friday morning, August 30, detectives Meyer and Clay drove to DFW Airport and boarded a flight to Annapolis. Their enthusiasm was minimal. But in the crazy world in which detectives live, they knew anything was possible.

After arrival, the cops from Texas drove their rental car up to Gate Number Eight at the Naval Academy, and identified themselves to the Marine Corps guards. They were expected, and in minutes a pair of Marine sergeants led Meyer and Clay through the gates and to the commandant's office, where he waited along with his legal adviser, Lieutenant Commander McCarthy. After introductions all around, the commandant excused himself in order to return to a pep rally, the first of the football season. McCarthy then escorted the detectives into a small meeting room, told them to have a seat, and directed the Marines to bring Plebe Zamora around.

Diane was in formation in Tecumseh Square, along with four thousand Middies yelling at the tops of their lungs, when a striper tapped her on the arm and pointed to the rear. She looked over her shoulder, where two Marines stood waiting with their arms folded. She asked the striper what was the problem. He said something in reply, but the band was playing too loudly for Diane to hear. Finally the striper leaned close and practically yelled, "I don't know, plebe. Orders are, you're to go with them."

Diane broke ranks and followed the Marines, as the band continued to blast "Anchors Aweigh" and the white-clad cheerleaders led the Navy goat into the center of the compound. On the way out of Tecumseh Square she passed Jenifer McKearney and Mandy Gotch. Both remained at attention and kept their gazes straight ahead.

The walk to the commandant's office begins at a door of solid oak, and continues down a corridor with a mirror-polished floor past coats of arms and paintings of admirals. The Marines kept Diane between them, their footsteps echoing from granite walls. They stopped a room down from the commandant's, where one guard peeked inside, then opened the door and ushered

Diane in. She entered, walking stiffly, dressed in starch-pressed whites. Lieutenant Commander McCarthy sat at a conference table with the detectives from Texas flanking him on either side. Though Diane was trembling, her plebe training took over and she snapped to attention to give a salute. McCarthy returned the salute, told the plebe to stand at ease, and then offered her a chair. Diane sat across the table from the Naval officer and the Grand Prairie detectives.

"These gentlemen are here to talk to you, Zamora." McCarthy gestured toward Meyer and Clay.

Diane's dark eyes shifted as she looked first at one detective and then the other.

McCarthy waited expectantly, his hands folded.

Clay looked at Meyer before he began. "Miss Zamora, we're Grand Prairie police, investigating the death of a Mansfield high school student last year. Adrianne Jones."

Clay and Meyer would later tell a Fort Worth magistrate that Diane showed little or no reaction when they first mentioned Adrianne's name. It's more likely that she was too stunned to speak. Clay went on, "Did you know Miss Jones?"

"No, I . . . Really, I didn't."

"Well," Clay said, "we're up here, frankly, because we heard different. According to what the people up here tell us, you've been going around saying that you killed her. Anything to that?"

"That I . . . ?" Diane managed a nervous laugh.

"Do you know David Graham, Miss Zamora?" Clay said.

Diane composed herself a bit. "David. Yes."

"Aren't the two of you engaged?"

"Well, we were. Yes, I guess we still are."

"This story we're hearing," Clay said, "is that you've told some people up here that you and David killed Adrianne Jones. Is that right?"

Diane made an attempt at sounding incredulous. "That David and me, that we killed somebody?"

Clay was growing more confident as the interview continued. "What we hear is, maybe David and Adrianne had something going together."

"David would never do that," Diane said. "Not with her."

Meyer now broke in. "Excuse me, a minute ago, you said that you didn't even know her."

Diane wet her lips. "Oh, that. Well, I didn't, but I read she got killed." She smiled as if something had occurred to her. "Look, I told those stories."

The detectives were careful here; they wanted no repeat performance of the James Drummond fiasco. "What stories are that, Miss Zamora?" Clay said.

"You know, those you were just talking about. That me and David killed her."

Clay leaned closer over the table, honing in. "Well, did you?"

"Did I . . . ?"

"You and David. Did you and David Graham kill Adrianne Jones, Miss Zamora?"

Diane had regained much of her composure. "I'll tell you about that. No, we didn't, but I did tell that to my roommates."

"Why would you say something like that if you didn't do it?"

Diane replied quickly, "I was just trying to sound like, I was tough, I guess. Just trying to impress them, I don't know why."

Meyer said, "You'd tell a story like that to *impress somebody*? Don't you know how funny that sounds to people."

Now Diane's look was crafty. "Maybe. But that's why I said it. It's all it means, I was just messing around. David and me, we would never do something like that. I was just trying to impress them. That's all, sir." She set her mouth in determination.

Throughout an interview session that lasted over two hours, Diane stuck to her guns. She didn't know anything about Adrianne Jones or who had killed her. She had read all about the murder, just as had everyone in north Texas, and she'd made up the story in order to impress her roommates. Switch gears as they might, asking trick questions, tripping her occasionally as to minute details, the detectives couldn't shake her story. They didn't have a shred of evidence against Diane Zamora, and without a confession they were no better off than they'd been before the Naval Academy had called Steve Noonkester in Mansfield.

There were, however, enough inconsistencies in what Diane had to say to convince the detectives that they were, at last, on to something. First she had denied ever hearing of Adrianne Jones, then, when questioned further, had stated that she'd read about the murder. Then, later on in the grilling session, she thought she might have *seen* Adrianne at a track meet, and another time she said David might have introduced them when Diane had visited him in Mansfield. Several times during the interview Meyer and Clay felt that Diane was on the edge of making a confession, but every time she seemed about to break, she would regroup and deny everything again.

Clay and Meyer finally terminated the interview in frustration. McCarthy then excused the plebe, and Diane returned to Bancroft Hall along with her escort of Marines.

McCarthy hadn't said a word during the entire question-and-answer session, and Meyer now asked the naval officer what he thought about Diane's responses.

McCarthy was deep in thought. Finally he said,

"Either she's lying about not being involved, or she was lying when she told the story to her roommates. Either way, she's lying. Liars aren't midshipman material, gentlemen. I'm sorry we haven't been more help in your murder investigation. But I'm afraid Miss Zamora is about to become someone's problem other than ours. And very quickly, if you know what I mean."

The detectives, though they had a possible break in one of the most brutal homicides in years, were not sure what they'd learned. They agreed with Lieutenant Commander McCarthy that Diane Zamora was lying, and have so stated in various affidavits filed in the current criminal case against David and Diane. Yet without a confession, they had no probable cause to arrest Diane—and indeed couldn't have arrested her without clearing a warrant through Maryland authorities, after which would have followed extradition proceedings. So the next step in their investigation was to talk to David and attempt to find contradictions between his story and hers.

It is well-known among homicide detectives that when one has suspects on the griddle, one strikes while the iron is hot. It was the Labor Day weekend, however. Meyer and Clay returned to Texas and took the next few days off. While they did, events occurred that muddied the cadet murder case even further.

* * *

Naval Academy officials didn't wait until after the holiday to take action where Diane was concerned. They didn't even wait until nightfall. No sooner had the Texas cops departed than McCarthy had a meeting with the commandant. They decided to handle things quickly but quietly, and at the same time to protect the Navy's flanks should Diane turn out to be innocent of the crime.

After the meeting, McCarthy had Diane brought to his office and placed her on indefinite leave, telling her to return to Texas until the murder investigation in which she had implicated herself was fully cleared. He then had the travel office issue Diane a U.S. Government Transportation Request for a plane ticket home, and dispatched two Marines to her room to pack her gear for her. The Marines escorted Diane to Baltimore-Washington Airport and put her on an evening Delta flight for DFW, with an hour's layover in Atlanta. As the Marines drove Diane, luggage and all, out the main gate of the Naval Academy, Lieutenant Commander McCarthy hoped that he had heard the last of the problem. He was to be gravely disappointed.

As naive as eighteen-year-old Diane Zamora might have been in the workings of the justice system, she didn't have any trouble at all in finding her way through Atlanta International Airport. Her Navy pay secure in her wallet, and her U.S. Government Transportation Request showing no restriction as to her destination, she made her way from counter to counter until she located an American flight to Colorado Springs with a layover in St. Louis. Because she was traveling in uniform, American Airlines had no reason to question her exchange of tickets, so off Diane flew to Colorado. Just as Labor Day weekend marks the first liberty for plebes at Annapolis after the grueling summertime training session, Air Force doolies have the holiday off as well.

The young lovers had three days in Colorado in which to rendezvous, make love, and get their stories straight.

When the Grand Prairie detectives returned to work after the holidays, they met with Chief Geary and then put in a call to the Air Force Academy. After a short delay they were put in touch with a legal officer. The detectives gave as little information as possible. First, they told the legal officer that they wanted to interview an Air force cadet, David Graham, as a possible witness to a crime. When pressed for details, the detectives finally said that the crime was a homicide. Had they outlined the purpose of their intended visit in detail, they might have had better results, but their conversation with the Air Force legal officer resulted in his calling in additional persons.

It is confusing enough for the average citizen that they are governed by two separate sets of laws, state and federal, but when one is a member of the armed forces, still a third group of statutes comes into play: the Uniform Code of Military Justice. While all three sets of laws are based on the U.S. Constitution, their codes of procedure are often quite different. For example, there is no federal murder statute—other than murders committed during violation of a drug law—and the UCMJ covers only crimes committed while one is in the military. So if the Grand Prairie cops had identified David as a Texas murder suspect to begin with, the Air Force would have permitted them to come to Colorado Springs and grill him to their hearts' content.

If David was merely a witness, however, he had certain rights that a suspect wouldn't have. Since he was now under military jurisdiction, David was not subject to a direct subpoena from the state of Texas for his testimony. The Air Force legal officer wasn't about to allow civilian cops to question David on a military installation without an armed services law enforcement officer present. They would be assisted by representatives from OSI.

OSI is short for Office of Special Investigations, and is probably best described as the military equivalent of the FBI. The difference between OSI and the Air Police is about the same—for our purposes, anyway—as the difference between city cops and the feds. Anytime there is a jurisdiction question on a military base, OSI comes in. OSI cops are members of the armed services—equally divided, in theory, between the Army, Navy, and Air Force—though they wear no uniforms and place no rank before their names. They remain anonymous in order to prevent suspects from pulling rank—as in the case of a sergeant investigating a general accused of sexual harassment, for example—and because the lead person on a case might be of a lower rank than his assistant.

The man and woman who greeted Meyer and Clay at the Colorado Springs airport, wearing civilian clothes, were persons from OSI's Denver office. The woman's name was Sheila and the man was Roy—what we know of these people's identities comes from David Graham's somewhat muddled memory. For reasons that will soon be obvious, the Office of Special Investigations, when queried about the interrogation of Air Force Academy cadet David Christopher Graham, will not furnish callers so much as the time of day.

We should keep in mind that portions of the following are based on David's memory, transmitted to us through his lawyers, and in weighing his truthfulness we should also remember that he stands charged in a grisly homicide. A good deal of the story is uncontested by police, however.

In order to conduct their interrogation, OSI and the Grand Prairie detectives borrowed the Air Police installation at the academy. This facility isn't much different from any other police station, albeit on a smaller scale, since the APs' duties usually consist of traffic regulation or busting the occasional drunk or stoned cadet on campus. The building, set on the southern half of the gorgeous campus, comes complete with an interview room that has a one-way mirror for outside observation purposes. The one-way mirror will have a later role in our story. The four cops, two from OSI and two from Texas, set up shop in the interview room. The Academy's fall term was underway, so a couple of AP's went out to bring the suspect in from class.

It should be stated that the courtroom donnybrook that will occur in pretrial over the admissibility of David's confession will have to do with the question of whether or not he was under arrest. Defense attorneys will argue that David was under arrest from the moment the AP's dragged him out of class; the prosecution will assert that the AP's were only escorting him over for a chitchat. The decision as to whether David was under arrest is a virtual toss-up, though in criminal matters the prosecution normally gets the nod when the judge can rule either way.

By now the Grand Prairie detectives had informed the OSI cops that David was much more than a potential witness, so the officers from OSI merely introduced themselves to the cadet and then let the men from Texas have the floor. David, obviously nervous and hugging himself, was dressed in fatigues and sat across from the four lawmen at a conference table. (David says that two AP's blocked his pathway to the exit, though for purposes of determining whether he was under arrest at the time, this is irrelevant; the issue is whether or not he was free to leave if he so desired.)

The Grand Prairie detectives weren't nearly as gentle as they'd been with Diane at Annapolis. Detective Meyer launched in: "You know why we're here, David. Don't you?"

David's expression was vacant, his gaze on something in the far corner of the room. "I can't say as I do, sir."

"Well, that's pretty easy to figure out, son." Meyer said. "We're here about Adrianne."

David recoiled as if punched in the solar plexus. "Adrianne? I don't know any—"

"Now, I'll tell you something," Meyer said, pointing a finger, "before you say another word. Diane's already told us everything, so trying to bullshit us is a waste of time."

Telling one suspect that another suspect has already confessed is, of course, as old as the hills—and one of the most effective interrogator's tricks as well. Under normal circumstances David might have given up the game right then and there. If defense attorneys are successful in having David's confession thrown out at trial, then Grand Prairie police will have their Labor Day holiday to blame. Unbeknownst to Clay and Meyer, David had just spent three days with Diane and knew very well that she hadn't admitted anything to the detectives. So instead of shaking the suspect, the old saw about the other perp already confessing bolstered David's confidence. His bullheadedness during the initial interview would set up the problem of his under-arrest status that would develop later on.

From that point forward, David was more relaxed. "I'm sorry, sir," he said. "But you must be mistaken. I don't know any Adrianne."

"Adrianne Jones, David," Meyer said. "You know who I'm talking about."

David even smiled. "I'm afraid I don't, sir. Is she someone I should know?"

Meyer was ready to blow his stack. "You know you killed her, David. You murdered her."

David looked to the OSI cops as if for an explanation. "Could somebody tell me what's going on here?"

There followed an intense—and to the policemen, frustrating—grilling session, which David says lasted for thirty hours, during which time he had nothing to eat and wasn't offered a rest period. The cops maintain that the interrogation was neither as long nor as grueling as David says it was, and the truth probably lies somewhere in between.

More pertinent to the issue of admissibility is David's assertion that he asked to see a lawyer during his initial interview. He says that when he asked for an attorney, OSI officer Sheila Bowen told him that his request would mean immediate dismissal from the Air Force Academy. The Grand Prairie police maintain that David never asked for a lawyer, and that he was never told any such thing. In sorting out conflicting stories, the judge is to consider what motives the parties might have for lying. David's incentive, of course, is to get out of jail. The policemen's motive is to keep their hard-earned confession in evidence, and while this is a greater incentive to lie than the public would like to believe, the cops are the favorite to win this issue even though David never signed the customary waiver of counsel.

At any rate, during interrogation, which was either (1) thirty hours—David's version—or (2) thirty minutes—the cops' estimation—in length, David didn't admit to a thing, though his story changed quite a bit along the way. He went from never having heard of Adrianne Jones to recalling her as a member of the cross-country team, to maybe having talked to her a time or two when she worked at the Golden Chicken, to having had sexual intercourse with her on a parking lot behind an elementary school. He likewise waffled on his experience with pistols—at first he didn't know a 9mm from a .22; later on he'd qualified on the firing range as an expert with five different handguns. His familiarity with the area around Joe Pool Lake kept changing as well. He went from not being certain if there was a lake near his hometown at all to knowing every back road around the shoreline. Through all of his inconsistencies, however, David remained steadfast on the major subjects; he had nothing to do with Adrianne Jones' murder and didn't have the slightest idea who could have been involved.

After what seemed an eternity of having David on the ropes, the Grand Prairie detectives were almost ready to give it up as a lost cause. Finally Clay said, "Tell you what, David. You willing to give us a polygraph?"

Clay has admitted in private that he never expected David to submit to a lie-detector test. Why should he? Polygraphs are helpful only to suspects in cases when the evidence is stacked against them.

David, his expression mild, answered, "Of course, sir. When would you like for me to?"

"Why, as soon as we can set it up, David," Clay

said. "We want to clear this up as bad as you do, son."

Polygraph examiners won't give a test until a day has passed since the suspect's interrogation. The theory is that without a calming-down period, a suspect's emotions might run amok and give a false reading to the lie detector. So the moment that David agreed to the test, the police terminated the interview. OSI then called in the Air Police, who placed David under house arrest until the following afternoon. It should be noted that this delay accounts for one of the days between September third and sixth.

At this point two questions have to be raised. First of all, why did David agree to the polygraph test? He'd avoided detection for nine months, and knew that the police had learned nothing from Diane with which to harm him. The working of the teenage mind—particularly of those who feel they have gotten away with something—defies all logic, so let's assume that David thought he might even fool the polygraph.

If David's decision was strange, however, that of the police to place him under arrest is very curious. At least David has the excuse that he was an eighteen-year-old with no experience in the justice system, but these were seasoned law enforcement officers. Possibly there was a miscommunication between the Grand Prairie detectives and the OSI reps. Whatever the reason, placing David under arrest was a strange move.

Here's why. As long as David wasn't under arrest, he wasn't legally entitled to a Miranda warning. But the moment the AP's took him to his quarters and placed a guard outside his door, the police had a duty to tell him he had a right to an attorney and failure to do so could void any confession he might give. It could be that the detectives had grown desperate at this point. They may have feared that if they advised him of his rights, he just might call for a lawyer and then there would go the polygraph examination.

Expect a full day in court during pretrial to deal with this matter. Prosecutors will ask questions such as, "Well, could he leave his room to go to the dining hall?", and to point out all the various freedoms David may have been granted during the twenty-four hours before he took the polygraph. Defense attorneys, on the other hand, will argue that house arrest is constructive arrest, and his confession isn't worth the paper it's written on.

In any case, David flunked the lie-detector test. Before we get to the test and its results, however, there was more police activity that was quite unusual and worth mentioning here.

After David had spent his night under house arrest, the AP's escorted him back to the interview room. To David's surprise, the Grand

Prairie detectives were nowhere in sight. Only the representatives from OSI were in the room, and the military officials at once informed him that Meyer and Clay had returned to Texas and that they, the OSI people, would be supervising his polygraph examination.

The OSI was lying. There was no way Meyer and Clay were going back to Texas before they learned the results of the lie-detector test. The truth was that the Grand Prairie cops were quite nearby. They were seated on the other side of the one-way mirror, and watching the proceedings inside the interview room with great interest. Just why the police resorted to bait-and-switch tactics in order to reel David in will probably never be known, but the answer may be nothing more than a question of jurisdiction. Policemen tend to guard their turf with the utmost rigor. The Grand Prairie cops had no authority on Air Force Academy grounds, and there might have been a decision made that if a cadet was to submit to a polygraph, he must do so under the aegis of military personnel. It's also quite possible that the switch was made only to fake David out, and the story told to him in hope that, with the Texas cops gone, he might think he was no longer under suspicion and be off his guard. For whatever reason, however, David went into his polygraph exam under the distinct impression that Meyer and Clay were hundreds of miles from Colorado.

* * *

After David finished taking his polygraph, he waited alone in the interview room until the OSI detectives got the results from the examiner. Finally, after an hour, the door burst open and the OSI people came in, walking fast. They sat across from David with the lie-detector graph in the center of the table, and looked the suspect in the eye. "You failed, Graham," one of the military cops said.

Visibly shaken, David squirmed in his chair and tried to look convincing. "There must be something wrong with the machine."

"No, there isn't. You responded to seven different questions about the murder, and in every instance the polygraph showed that you were lying." The OSI detective intertwined fingers on the table in bargaining posture. "Make it easy on yourself, Graham. Give it up."

David was suddenly chilled and unable to swallow. He looked at the detective, then at the polygraph paper, and back at the detective again. "Can I see a lawyer now?" he finally said.

The rest is all David's story. He says that when he asked for a lawyer—for the second time since confronted by Grand Prairie cops at the Air Force Academy—the OSI people responded with false concern. He was eligible for probation in this case, but if he got a lawyer, they were almost certain to give him the death penalty. It strains credibility that the cops would tell him he was more likely to receive a death penalty without a lawyer than with one—or that David would swallow such a story—but David insists that is what he was told. Whatever the OSI people in fact said to David, it's likely that if he did ask for an attorney at that point, they did try to talk him out of seeing one. Even with the failed lie-detector test in their possession, police were far from having anything with which to proceed in the case. Lack of counsel becomes critical for David at this point, because the results of lie-detector tests are inadmissible as evidence in a courtroom.

He didn't get a lawyer, however, and though he refused to sign a waiver of counsel, it will be his word against the police's as to whether he asked for an attorney. The OSI people then began a furious interrogation that lasted the rest of the day, and sometime in the duration detectives Clay and Meyer emerged from their hiding place behind the one-way mirror.

Around nightfall, David gave it up. He admitted to the murder and, his hands trembling in the relief that always accompanies such confessions, agreed to tell the story of the killing from start to finish. And so while it was Diane Zamora speaking out at the Naval Academy that furnished the break in the case, it was David Graham's confession in Colorado that sealed their doom. Diane and David may now live whatever lives remain in store for them with the knowledge that they are equally to blame for their downfall.

Once David confessed verbally to the crime, the police had probable cause to make an arrest, but now ran into a jurisdiction problem of a different nature. David had committed no offense under the Uniform Code of Military Justice, so the OSI detectives had no reason to detain him, and the Grand Prairie policemen couldn't take him into custody without a warrant from Texas being forwarded to the Colorado Springs authorities. The Air Police held David at the station while Meyer and Clay did the paperwork, faxing a probable-cause statement to Texas, then waiting a couple of hours until the warrant, executed by a Texas judge, was faxed to the Colorado Springs Police Department. That accomplished, the detectives handcuffed David, drove him from the academy into town, and booked him into the El Paso County Jail after dark on Friday, September 6.

There is an odd fact about criminal suspects who have held their silence for long periods of time. Once they decide to confess, they are often willing to tell more than policemen need to hear in order to make a case against them. David was no exception. Since all the police stenographers had taken off for the weekend, Meyer and Clay alternated on a borrowed typewriter in an office at the jail while David rambled on and on. At one point David took over the typing himself because the detectives weren't moving fast enough for him. Eventually the detectives edited the statement to four-and-a-half pages, which David eventually signed, but even the finished product could use some slimming down. It is punctuated over and over with asides, most of which have to do with David's passion for Diane and how his guilt drove him to commit the crime, and many of his expressions of love are sophomoric and a bit on the corny side.

Through it all, though, a story clearly emerges. The tale of bloody murder chilled even the hardened cops who had to listen. The murder allegedly committed by David Graham and Diane Zamora was nothing short of horrifying.

# 13

The pistol was a Marakov, made in Russia. Its bore is nine millimeters in diameter, and it fires a high-velocity shell big enough to stop a charging bull. If not properly braced when fired, the gun delivers a kick sufficient to send its shooter to the hospital. David's Marakov was stowed inside a tote bag placed on the rear floorboard of Diane Zamora's Mazda hatchback. Also inside the bag was a twenty-five-pound dumbbell freeweight and two ankle weights. The weights collided with the pistol whenever the Mazda went over a dip in the road, giving out a series of dull metallic clunks.

It was a ten-minute drive from Cedar Street, where David lived, to the Jones home. To reach their destination, Diane and David skirted the back of the Mansfield City Hall onto Broad Street, drove down Broad past the Golden Chicken and Erma Nash Elementary School, and turned left onto Walnut Street a block the other side of Main. Diane and David barely spoke to each other on the trip, passing the bourbon back and forth and taking swigs, shoring up their nerve. It was after midnight, and the temperature had dipped into the fifties. The small town was practically deserted and its streetlights dim.

Walnut is a two-lane street that is wide enough for four lanes, and the Jones home was on David's left as he turned the Mazda off Broad. He passed his destination and made a U-turn in order to park at the curb directly in front of the house, and killed the engine. The couple sat in silence for a moment and treated themselves to a final slug of whiskey.

Finally David nodded to Diane that he was ready. At his signal she scrambled over the seat into the back, then wriggled up and over once again until she settled into the narrow space beneath the hatchback. David got out and crossed the yard to the front of the house. He hesitated, moved to his left, trotted into the shadow cast by the stockade fence, and disappeared from view.

Diane trembled in anticipation as she lay wedged under the Mazda's hatchback, shutting her eyes tightly and stoking her hatred for a girl she'd never even met before. Her arms ached and her knees cramped within the tiny space, but she remained as still as a stone.

In a few moments the sound of female laughter

reached her ears as Adrianne approached the car. The front passenger door opened, then closed with a thud, followed by a tilting sensation as body weight shifted in the seat. Then David got in, his greater bulk shifting the weight back to the other side. The engine caught and raced. Then the car pulled into the street. Diane heard the clink of glass and the sound of someone drinking from a bottle. Adrianne laughed and said something Diane couldn't make out, and David's deep-voiced reply was unintelligible as well. The car tilted again as David made the right turn onto Broad, and then Adrianne laughed again at something that David said. Diane gritted her teeth and kept her silence as the Mazda rattled its way down Broad Street.

Persons imprisoned for planned acts of violence have said that just before the moment of truth, a strange detachment takes over. The sensation is not unlike dreaming, a feeling as if one is watching from a distance while events occur that are out of one's control.

David Graham drove slowly out of town to the east, all the way out Broad Street until it became a country road between farms and land staked out for subdivisions. The path he took was aimless and without purpose; though he'd planned the site very carefully with Diane, he suddenly realized that he was lost. All the backroads between Mansfield and the lake have a sameness about them, and travelers often see familiar things around hairpin turns—a sign, perhaps, or maybe cylindrical hay bales in a field—which make them feel as if they've doubled back and are retracing their steps. David and Diane had planned to kill Adrianne near the lake, tie the weights to her body, and sink her into the depths, but David wasn't sure in which direction lay the water.

He bore to his left, down a narrow blacktop road with barely room for two autos to pass abreast. Adrianne, barefoot, wearing a long-sleeve pullover over running shorts, sat relaxed in the seat with the bottle upright between her thighs. Early in the drive she'd chatted incessantly. Now she seemed to have caught the mood of the night, and gazed mutely out the window at scrubby trees and underbrush. The road ahead crested and graded downward. David slowed, switched on the parking lights, and peered ahead for a likely place to pull to the side.

He was at the bottom of the grade, leveling out, when dim shapes of mailboxes loomed on his right. He passed an opening in a fence on his left, a cattle guard enclosed by twin iron tripods. He braked, reversed, and spun the wheel to the left as he backed up onto the cattle guard. There was a scraping noise as the single strand of barbed wire over the opening grazed the Mazda's bumper. David jammed the lever into Park, cut the engine, and turned off the lights. Adrianne smiled at him, pressing the side lever to lay the seat back, raising the bottle to her lips in order to take a pull.

She froze in shock at a scrambling noise from the backseat. She turned with her lips parted as the car rocked on its springs, and a small girl tumbled out from beneath the hatchback, hit the seat rolling, and struggled up into a sitting position. Adrianne looked at the girl, then at David, and back again; understanding dawned in Adrianne's expression even though it was now too late for her. In her last seconds of life Adrianne Jones no doubt pictured Kimberly Horton, her best friend, as Lindsay Wade raised her baseball bat to beat her.

Diane leaned forward and got up in Adrianne's face. Pointing toward David, Diane screamed, "That's my boyfriend, bitch. You been fucking my boyfriend, bitch?" Her hand went to the floorboard and dipped inside the tote bag.

What happened then neither David nor Diane had expected. Instead of cowering in terror, Adrianne twisted her features into an expression of hatred. She pushed away from the door and came across the seat at David, punching, hitting him in the face, clawing him with her nails.

The surprise attack caught David off guard, and all he could do was raise his hands in a defensive posture. A small fist landed a blow to the side of his head, and a sharp nail gashed his cheek. Adrianne started screaming obscenities, her saliva spraying David's face. "You son of a bitch! You *fucker*, you!"

In the backseat, Diane grunted with exertion as she raised the dumbbell weight over her head. She swung blindly, bringing the weight down hard on the seat back in front of her. Once, twice, three times she swung the twenty-five pounder, each time missing her target. Her forearms ached with the effort as Adrianne continued to shriek and punch and flail at David.

Diane sucked in breath as she regrouped one final time. She raised the weight, blood rushing into her cheeks, her pulse pounding in her throat. With all her strength she brought twenty-five pounds of steel crashing down onto the side of Adrianne Jones's head.

This time she connected. There was a sound like a bat striking a ripe melon. Adrianne's head snapped to one side, recoiled, then flopped loosely on her neck as blood gushed, pouring from the wound. Adrianne sagged in the seat, writhing and moaning.

The lovers stared at each other across the seat back while their victim's lifeblood drained. A full minute passed. David nodded to Diane, then grabbed Adrianne's shoulders and prepared to lift her out of the car.

Suddenly Adrianne moved, putting her hands against David's chest and shoving away from him. As Diane and David sat dumbstruck, Adrianne went through the open passenger window. Squirming, her legs pistoning, she tumbled headlong down the side of the Mazda and rolled over on the ground. Then, incredibly, with blood matting her hair and streaming across her temple into her eyes, Adrianne was up and running. She dodged this way and that in a mindless panic, starting across the road, doubling back, taking two long strides until she reached the barbed-wire fence, then tumbled over the fence into the field. Barbs ripped the flesh on her legs. She lay on the ground just inside the fence, writhing and twisting not thirty steps from where David and Diane sat, too stunned to move, inside the car.

Finally Diane hissed, "We can't let her get away, David. You've got to go after her."

His movements wooden, David got out of the car and approached the fence, feeling a cool breeze on his cheeks. Adrianne was on her back now, her arms and legs outspread like a crucifix victim's. Her face was turned to the side, the wound in her head a coal black gash in the moonlight. David turned away from the sight, walked slowly back to the car, and leaned in through the window. "She's dead," he said breathlessly. "I think she's dead."

Diane glanced past him toward the body.

"She's moving. I can see her move." Diane bent over, rummaged inside the tote bag, and brought the Marakov pistol up by its barrel. She offered David the gun, handle first. "We have to finish her, David," she said.

David clenched his jaw, took the pistol, and went back over to the fence. He stepped over the wire and straddled the body, a tall young soldier in fatigues and combat boots, held the gun in both hands in a classic shooter's pose, and placed the barrel less than a foot from Adrianne's face. At the last instant he looked away and tightly shut his eyes. Then, a sob escaping from his lips, David squeezed the trigger. Two loud blasts shattered the night as the Marakov bucked in his hands, the echoes bouncing from the road, over the fields, all the way to Joe Pool Lake and back again.

After David signed his confession, Meyer and Clay turned him over to El Paso County deputies, who led him away and locked him in a private maximum-security cell. Those who have confessed to crimes agree that the relief that floods over them after they'd gotten things off their chests is unbelievable, as if the weight of the world has been lifted from their shoulders. David hasn't remarked on his own feelings, but once he reached his cell he slept for fifteen hours and, upon awakening, wolfed down two large helpings when breakfast was served.

Though they were doubtless as exhausted as the prisoner, Meyer and Clay had more work to do. They filled out reports and faxed them, along with a copy of David's confession, back to Grand Prairie, and held a long-distance conference call with Deputy Chief Geary and some cops over in Mansfield. All agreed that, at long last, the investigation into the murder of Adrianne Jones was finally over. Then Meyer and Clay, tired to the bone, went to their motel room and turned in themselves. Just how long the detectives slept isn't known. But they missed their flight home the following day and had to remain at the Colorado Springs airport for several hours, taking pot luck on standby until they finally boarded a later plane.

Meanwhile, back in Fort Worth, Diane had lied to her parents. Her explanation for her return home from the Naval Academy—that she'd witnessed a crime in her dorm and that officials had placed her on leave while the matter was under investigation—was rather lame, and Carlos and Gloria likely wouldn't have believed her if they'd thought about it, but the Zamoras had major problems of their own. They had been evicted from their house, and were bunking in with Miguel Mendoza down the street from El Templo de Juan. During the week between her return from the academy and her arrest, Diane slept on the couch in her grandfather's living room.

With a copy of David's confession in hand via fax, Grand Prairie police had no problem in securing a probable-cause warrant for Diane's arrest. David entered the jail in Colorado Springs on Friday night, and by Saturday afternoon police in Texas were ready to pick up Diane. Interestingly, whereas they'd gone after James Drummond with SWAT teams and shotgun squads, Grand Prairie's finest were meek as lambs in arresting one of the real killers. Around three o'clock two plainclothes detectives knocked politely on Miguel Mendoza's door and asked for Diane Zamora, then escorted her without leg restraints or handcuffs to the unmarked sedan waiting at the curb, and held the door for her. There was no hoopla involved in booking Diane, no press or photographers waiting as she walked into the Grand Prairie City Jail, turned her valuables in at the desk, and allowed uniformed guards to lock her quietly into a private cell.

Detectives allowed Diane to cool her heels for an hour or so, then had her brought up front into an interview room. There will be no question at trial as to the legality of Diane's confession—other than a prompting issue, which we'll get to in a minute—since detectives were very careful in handling her. The cops first advised her of her rights and asked her if she wanted to speak to a lawyer. She declined and signed a waiver of counsel; she knew very well what was coming, and was ready to get it over with. When shown a copy of David's confession she barely glanced at the page (there is a suspicion that between his arrest and hers, David had called Diane from the jail in Colorado and told her what to expect), then informed detectives that she was ready to give a statement of her own. The policemen then called in a stenographer, and Diane began to speak. As she dictated her statement, one of the detectives followed along with a copy of David's confession in his lap. According to Diane, every time her story differed from David's in the slightest, the detective would stop her, read her what David had to say, and then allow her to make corrections with the stenographer. If this sort of editing did occur, then the fact that Diane Zamora's description of the murder is identical to David's description is not the near miracle that, on the surface, it might appear to be.

# 14

"Andy and Barney," Dan Cogdell says, "need to get their shit together." He's sitting in his office overlooking downtown Houston, and he's speaking of the gang from Mayberry, from the old *Andy Griffith Show.*

"See, what you've got here," Cogdell says, waving his hand at two huge evidence folders he's received from the Tarrant County District Attorney's Office, "is the biggest bullshit confession I've ever run across, and I've seen a few." Which Cogdell has; prominent on the wall behind him is a framed newspaper headline reading "Branch Davidians Acquitted in San Antonio Trial," with his own photo above the story text as he and his client square off with reporters for an interview. It isn't the only case Cogdell has won; it's only the most famous, as he builds a reputation that stands alongside legendary Houston lawyers such as Percy Foreman and Richard (Racehorse) Haynes.

"Exactly what's wrong with the confession?" the interviewer says.

"Well, get this picture," Cogdell says, spreading hands with perfectly manicured nails. "Here you got Andy and Barney from the Grand Prairie police department, driving their beat-up old heap up to the Air Force Academy and hooking up with Bilko and Pyle, two more comedians in the act. Then they haul this kid who's never been away from home in his life, they haul him outta class and grill him thirty hours straight. Two times"—Cogdell shows upraised fingers—"the boy asks for a lawyer, and what answer have Bilko and Pyle got for that one? Well, first they tell him if he gets a lawyer, he's immediately kicked outta the Air Force Academy. Second time they say if he gets a lawyer, he's gonna get the death penalty, can you believe it? Illegal, inadmissible, and downright stupid."

This is a man who cannot stand to lose. He once showed his dedication for his client by shocking himself with a cattle prod. True story. He was defending a man in Kerrville, in the center of the Texas hill country, who prosecutors claimed had killed another man by torturing him with a cattle prod until the victim had a heart attack.

"Hurt like a sonofabitch," Cogdell says, rubbing his upper arm and wincing at the memory. "But my guy didn't cause the death, no way. And look, the jury only saw it a couple of times. I sat up in my hotel room, practicing, and shocked myself with that thing until my hair was standing straight up in the air. See, I had to keep grinning all the while I was doing this, so the jury could see it didn't hurt so bad, so I'm standing there with this grin on my face and feeling like screaming, 'Oh, Jesus' or something. But, hey, it worked, didn't it?"

His client got off with seven years' probation for assault, and Cogdell today keeps the cattle prod inside a glass case in his office.

"I'll tell you something about taking cases for publicity," Cogdell says. "It works some ways, and it doesn't work some ways. I defended that guy"—here he points at the Branch Davidian headline on the wall behind him—"for free, and it damn near cost me everything. Months in trial, no income, my wife left me to boot, and hey, I won the case, but by the time it was over I couldn't even afford to pay my secretary. I come into it, here's my client in the burn unit up in Dallas, and the first time I visit him we see on television how his wife didn't survive that fire in Waco, and right in the middle of our talk he's breaking down in tears. So the feds have burned this man damn near to death, killed his wife, and now they want to throw his ass in jail. So you think I'm going to sit there and quote this man a fee I know he can't pay? Hell, no, I'm not. I'm going to defend this man, and if it gets my name in the paper, good for me."

The Branch Davidian's name was Clive Doyle, and those who followed the trial in San Antonio credit Cogdell not only with his own client's defense, but with the acquittals of several others of the cult as well. "They had them all in the same pot," says San Antonio lawyer Joseph Philmer, "and what was evidence against one was evidence against the others. Every day it was Cogdell on the attack, and when he spoke for Doyle he was talking for the other Davidians, too. That day he told the press that the prosecutor didn't have the testosterone to put some witness on because Cogdell would eat the witness for lunch on cross, I thought he was in for it with the bar association and everybody else in the state. Not one lawyer in a thousand could get away with what he did down there, but he's the one and my hat's off to him."

In connection with the Davidian case, Cogdell has a word to say about gratitude. "Now, Clive Doyle is a good and religious man, but enough got to be enough. After his acquittal we cross the street to this hotel where we're staying, and Doyle's giving his press conference while I'm about twenty feet away bellied up to the bar, okay? So while I'm throwing down a few scotches, here's my client telling the newspapers over and over"—and here Cogdell strikes an evangelist's pose—" 'I thank God and David Koresh for this day.' I'm not kidding you. 'I thank God and David Koresh.' All these guys, they think David Koresh is going to rise up out of the ashes someday and smite the enemy or something, right?

"So right in the middle of all this," Cogdell says, "I get about half a snootful, and about the fiftieth time I'm hearing the credit going to God and a dead man, I can't take it anymore. So I go over and sort of nudge my client outta the way, and there I am in this circle of reporters and TV people waving a scotch and water, right? So I gotta say something, I've busted up my client's news conference and everything, so the first thing that pops in my head is, 'The last time I checked, neither God nor David Koresh has a license to practice law in this state. So he can thank God and David all he wants, but he'd better save some gratitude for me, okay?' My client's never spoken to me since, but maybe someday I'll rise out of the ashes and save his ass again, you think so?"

There is a method in Cogdell's madness. He strikes an impressive figure, tall, slim, and impeccably dressed, but there is a fierce concentration about the eyes. Cogdell lives and breathes the practice of criminal law, and when he's not sitting at the defense table during trial, sizing up the opposition or taking the floor himself with razor-sharp questions that often make prosecution witnesses squirm on the stand, you're apt to find

Cogdell burning the midnight oil in the law library with his nose in a book. Even his detractors—and there are lawyers who bristle at Cogdell's open courting of the limelight—confess that he is as apt a student of the law as one will find anywhere in America.

"It works like this," he says. "These people in the D.A.'s office don't know shit about the law, because they've never had to dig it out for themselves. If they got a question, say about some recent decisions or something, all they got to do is call up one of the five thousand law clerks they got running around over there and send 'em into the library. Then the prosecutor gets a brief laid out on his desk which he's never even read before, and if he's got to argue that same brief in front of the judge, he's out in left field. My side's always taking the worst of it to begin with, so I've got to know what I'm talking about. So I do know. I make it a point to know.

"You take this kid here," Cogdell says, "and this half-assed confession they wrung out of him. With all this publicity going around, it's going to be hard for a judge to take the heat of throwing out the confession even if the judge knows the law isn't in his corner. So we're sort of like, playing the Aggies in College Station, where the referees are gonna throw the flag on you every time you turn around.

"Under Texas law"—and here Cogdell's diction

shifts as he assumes a teaching attitude—"I've got three opportunities to combat this confession. First at the suppression hearing held in pretrial in front of the judge, and we're not kidding ourselves that isn't a tough row to hoe. First of all, it's a given that the police are gonna take the stand and lie about what went on up there. It's one reason I've been so vocal in the press about this. The Grand Prairie police leaked my client's confession to the *Dallas Morning News* the day after he gave it, then the *News* claims they didn't get the confession from the police, but we know better, right? They've sort of hinted they might have gotten the confession from the Air Force people, but hey, come on. The Air Force doesn't have a horse in this race. I wouldn't be surprised if Grand Prairie didn't fax a copy to the *Dallas Morning News* at the same time they sent it back to headquarters. Anyway, we're not living in a dream world here, and though we'll fight like hell at the pretrial hearing, we're going under the assumption that the judge is going to admit the confession." Cogdell winks broadly before saying, "But even if he does, we're not through.

"The second avenue under the law," Cogdell says, "is during jury voir dire. I get to ask each and every one of them, say, Mr. or Mrs. prospective juror, if you believe that my client's confession was illegally obtained, can you disregard the confession and render a decision based on whatever other evidence you may hear? That of course is sort of a frivolous question, because every prospective juror—except for the ones looking for an excuse to beg off the panel anyway, and we can't do anything about those people—will answer in the affirmative even if in truth it's impossible for them to disregard something the court's permitted them to hear. But it plants a seed in their minds, and all it takes is one"—here Cogdell raises a finger—"one ever loving sweetheart to stick to their guns during deliberations, and the state can't get a conviction.

"And finally," Cogdell says, "assuming I can get anything into evidence that the police took David's confession illegally—and this doesn't rule out putting my client on the stand, though I'm not ready to talk about that can of worms just yet—I can get into it on closing argument and ask the judge for a jury instruction that if the panel believes the confession is tainted, they may disregard it altogether. That's three shots, which is better than no shots at all. We're not beaten until the gun sounds. I'm *never* beaten until the gun sounds."

The interviewer can't keep the skepticism out of his voice. "Isn't it unrealistic to think, with all the publicity, with the confession printed in the newspapers, that your client has a real chance of acquittal in this case?"

Cogdell's eyes flash with competitive fire. "No,

it's not unrealistic, and if I didn't think I could win this case I wouldn't be sitting here doing this. Not unrealistic at all."

Cogdell is peddling uphill against a strong wind and knows it, but there's something in his attitude which makes one believe that anything is possible. He's done it before, and certainly studied at the feet of a master. After his upbringing in a Houston suburb and four years at the University of Texas in Austin, touring sorority row and Sixth Street nightclubs—"I graduated with something like a two-point-oh-oh-oh-oh-one," Cogdell says—he returned to his hometown without much direction in his life other than a desire to eat and a passion for racing motorcycles.

"I drank a lot and I got married a lot [three times, all ending in divorce], but I was always taken with lawyer stories. Thomas Thompson's book, *Blood and Money*, I must have read it five times, and the story just captured me." Here he's talking about Thompson's marvelous chronicling of Houston's most famous murder defense, wherein a high-profile society doctor was charged with poisoning his wife, was represented by the legendary Racehorse Haynes at trial and acquitted, and was later gunned down in his River Oaks mansion by hit men allegedly contracted by his father-in-law, though there was never enough evidence to take the father-in-law to trial. "And then racing motorcycles I met Race in person, and the man was bigger in life than he was in the book. I was hooked. I was going to be a lawyer if it killed me."

It so happens that Houston is home to the only night law school in the Lone Star State. South Texas College of Law is no Harvard or Yale—it's downtown, in an area where many students tote weapons for protection—but it boasts among its graduates some of the finest criminal-defense minds in the country. Houston, in fact, has more high-profile criminal attorneys per capita than any city in the world, and to the man they worked at one time either for Percy Foreman—who defended Candace Mossler in the fifties and, later, represented James Earl Ray, cutting Ray a deal that saved him from the death penalty after the Martin Luther King assassination—or Racehorse Haynes. Cogdell clerked for Haynes while in law school and, upon graduation, quickly became Racehorse's right-hand man. He left Haynes in 1990 to begin his own practice, and Haynes says today that he still considers Cogdell a surrogate son.

Oddly, David Graham, once he'd assessed his situation in the El Paso County Jail, put in a call to his mother, even though he'd lived exclusively with his father ever since his parents' separation. Janice Graham had departed Mansfield in May of

1996—the day after David's high school graduation—for a teaching job in the Houston suburb of Spring. After inquiries as to the best man available to defend her son, Janice arrived on Cogdell's doorstep. Though they continue to live apart, Janice and Jerry Graham are still married and jointly pay their son's legal expenses. Cogdell's fee is no one's business other than his and the Grahams', but it suffices to say that Janice and Jerry are a teacher and a retired principal respectively. Cogdell certainly has more lucrative clients—in January of this year he began the defense of a doctor whose controversial cancer treatments have spawned clinics around the country—but to his credit, his defense of David Graham is every bit as vigorous as it would be if David owned a chain of hotels.

Still, however, with the confession at the forefront of every major newspaper story about the case, David's problems are more than serious even with his parents firmly behind him and a certified legal magician in his corner. Many experts feel that extricating David from the mess he's in would be a task worthy of a Hollywood stuntman. Well, the fact is, in addition to his own expertise, Cogdell, believe it or not, employs a stuntman as well.

In *Robocop II*, shot while Rob Swofford was in college, Rob drove motorcycles through hails of bullets and fell off horses. He's active in the Houston Stuntman's Association even today, though now he spends most of his time in the courtroom or getting ready for trial.

Like his boss and mentor, Dan Cogdell, Rob Swofford is a native of Houston. Rob grew up diving off everything from low boards to platform towers, and by the time he graduated from high school he had several offers of athletic scholarships. Yet if he went to college on scholarship, that meant he had to maintain his amateur status. If he accepted money for stunt diving, he could lose his eligibility to compete in NCAA events. So he paid his way to Baylor University and existed on what work he could drum up in diving exhibitions and movie roles. The latter were hard to come by, but he made pretty good money during the summer when *Robocop II* had its filming in Houston. The interviewer asks him if he feels that the scene where Robocop blows Swofford and a couple of other villians away with one blast from his rocket gun is one of the finest moments ever captured on film.

"Well, not really," he says, laughing. "It was fun and all that, but trying to make a living in stunt work is almost impossible without the right connections. Actors get breaks, try out for parts, and maybe the right one comes along, but stunt people have to know somebody. I didn't know anyone, so I went to law school."

So much was the film business in his blood that

Swofford wanted to be an entertainment lawyer. "I had no idea of ever practicing criminal law," he says, "but sort of stumbled into it doing intern work in Houston during breaks in law school. Trial work, addressing juries, is a lot the same as performing, so here I am."

Swofford looks studious at first glance, with a smooth, intelligent face behind wire-framed glasses, but he keeps in shape and maintains the thick, muscular body of a platform diver. His wife is an attorney as well, with a downtown Houston civil firm.

Actually, Swofford was David Graham's first contact with legal assistance in Colorado. Cogdell was in trial elsewhere when retained on the case, and Swofford flew to Colorado Springs in order to handle the new client's extradition proceedings. David remained in Colorado for two weeks after his arrest before finally waiving extradition and allowing Tarrant County deputy sheriffs to escort him back to Texas.

"Fighting extradition in the long run is pointless," Swofford says, "because if your client is wanted in another jurisdiction, eventually they're going to extradite the guy. But you can learn a lot in those extradition hearings about the case they have against you, because the other side has to come up with some kind of probable cause for the charges. I learned a lot about David and his case while I was up there, and picked up a few things from the Air Force Academy people that we very likely can use. So we learned what we could and then we waived extradition. All in all, the experience was worth the trip."

Does Swofford share Cogdell's feelings about the confession? "You bet. You dig out every piece of case law regarding illegally obtained confessions, and this one's the model. If you're under arrest, the police can't so much as say hello to you without giving you Miranda and obtaining a waiver of counsel. And David was under arrest. The Air Force cops are law enforcement people, and house arrest is arrest, period. It doesn't matter under the law if you're in another jurisdiction, and David was detained about the very case they've charged him with, the murder. They can explain it, twist it around any way they want to, but *they* arrested him. We didn't. The confession was illegally obtained."

In the upcoming trial of the case entitled *State of Texas* v. *David Christopher Graham*, barring the confession would have a far wider impact than just David's description of the murder. Acting on information obtained from David, police descended on the Graham home in Mansfield armed with a warrant and conducted a search. In the attic they located a 9mm Russian-made Marakov pistol. Ballistics people matched it to the shells and casings found near Adrianne's body at the crime scene. Plus, they found a box containing a dumbbell weight encrusted with Adrianne's blood. Both of these items are fruits of David's confession, and if the confession is thrown out, the physical evidence is out as well. Without the confession David could very well walk, and law enforcement people tread very lightly when approaching this issue. David's defense attorneys, however, are happy to discuss the confession at length.

"Don't you think it's strange," Cogdell says, "that the weaker the case, the more evidence gets leaked to the newspapers? They know what shape they're in with David's alleged statement, so they want to make sure everybody reads about it and that the jurors will know about the confession even if they don't hear it in trial. They can talk about gag orders all they want to, but before a judge can gag everybody, the information's already out. So if the police can go around trying the case in the paper, why can't I?"

And if the confession gets in?

Cogdell leans back, pensive. "Then we'll go to plan B, which we haven't thought of as yet. Maybe my client wasn't even there and he's protecting his girlfriend. Maybe David was off in South America promoting a drug deal. But we'll do a good job defending this kid, that you can count on. It's what we're here for, and that's what we're going to do."

# 15

Fort Worth is where the West begins, where men are men and where the annual Rodeo and Fat Stock Show continues to outdraw the Dallas Cowboy games. Bowlegged men in boots and Stetson hats are common sights downtown even today, as are women in buckskin shirts with rawhide fringes on the sleeves, and the natives all seem to be distantly related. In the midst of all this yesteryear charm and good-ole-boy surroundings, David Graham and Diane Zamora will go on trial later this year.

The criminal legal community is a tightly knit group in any major city, but in Fort Worth the situation is even more so. Many of the lawyers have known each other since they were knee-high to tadpoles. Some are married to sisters, and some to ex-wives of other lawyers around town. Carlos Zamora's retention of an attorney in Diane's behalf is typical of Fort Worth goings-on.

John Linebarger headed out for a dinner party

over in Dallas one Saturday night, left his wife to cool her heels inside the car for a couple of hours, and picked up Diane as a client along the way. As Linebarger tells it, "I have my office phones forwarded to my car on weekends, and here we are on I-30, just pulling abreast of Six Flags, when the car phone buzzes. I came within a hair of not answering it, to tell you the truth, but when I picked up, here's the most haunted voice I've ever heard telling me his daughter's in the Grand Prairie City Jail charged with murder. I look up just about then, and doggone if the next freeway exit doesn't lead to Grand Prairie. So I pull off the interstate, drive on over to the jail, and tell my wife I'll be out in fifteen minutes or so. Well, it's two hours later when I finally get back, that's how much the story took a hold of me, and I'll tell you something. This is no killer. This little girl is no killer. I don't care what they say."

"Did you ever make the dinner party?" the interviewer says.

Linebarger smiles. "The food was cold."

"Is your wife still speaking to you?"

"She's used to it. Being married to a lawyer, she never knows what's next. But she's used to it."

With a telephone book full of federal drug defendants as a client list, it's difficult for Linebarger himself to know what's next. He does quite well in his practice and normally shuns publicity.

"If anyone had told me before I got into this"—he's talking about Diane's defense—"what all it was going to entail, and I hadn't met the client, I doubt I would have been interested."

"You mean, when you got the call, you'd never even heard of the case?" the interviewer asks.

"No way." Linebarger is emphatic, gesturing with his hands. "You've got to remember, they arrested David in Colorado on a Friday, then picked up Diane at her grandfather's on Saturday afternoon, and it was Monday before all the news hounds got the word. When I stopped off at the Grand Prairie jail, I didn't even know she'd been an Annapolis student. As far as I knew, this was a shooting during a hold-up they were charging her with." He shakes his head in puzzlement. "This intelligent young lady was something I wasn't expecting."

Diane, incidentally, has an aunt who works for a Tarrant County judge, which may give some idea of what a small world that Fort Worth, Texas, really is. It was the aunt who referred Carlos Zamora to Linebarger in the first place.

"When did you first realize you were into something big?"

"By Monday afternoon," Linebarger says, pointing toward his reception area, "that phone out there was ringing every other minute, and my regular clients couldn't get through to me. *Time, Newsweek, People,* you name it. Wanted to interview me, my client, my client's parents, neighbors, whoever. I had my assistant keep a log. A hundred calls a day, I'm not kidding you. It ticks me off that there have been things in the paper like, that I've got Androvet because I'm some publicity freak. I've got Androvet for one reason, to keep the newspapers off my ass so I can practice law."

Androvet as in Mike, a former Channel 5 television reporter who became somewhat of a local celebrity himself—he has a law degree and hosted the O.J. Simpson trial telecasts in 1995—before starting his own media-relations firm. His clients are for the most part lawyers in similar situations to Linebarger's—though in 1996 he represented a witness in the drug trial of Dallas Cowboys star Michael Irvin—for whom he runs interference with the press. Today if newspeople call about Diane Zamora, Linebarger's staff refers the reporters to Androvet's office.

John Linebarger, a slim forty-nine-year-old with a laid-back courtroom manner, is a hundred percent homegrown, from Pascal High to Texas Wesleyan University. He took a roundabout path to becoming an attorney. He was an aspiring teacher, and after getting a bachelor's degree began to take graduate courses at TCU. While studying for his master's during the day, he became a night patrolman with the sheriff's department. He'd neglected to include sleep in his schedule, however, and grad school soon fell by the wayside. Linebarger became a full-time sheriff's deputy. He moved up rapidly within the department, passed the detectives' test, and within two years became an investigator with the district attorney's office.

"Best experience I could have for what I do now," he says. "Prosecutors do strictly the legal work, but it's the investigators who compile the evidence. So in the courtroom, when I see what's laid out against my client, I've got a better idea where it all came from than the ADA prosecuting the case. It helps. Believe me, it helps."

So much did he shine as a D.A.'s investigator that the head man himself told Linebarger that if he could get a law license, there was always a place for him in Tarrant County. Linebarger took the D.A. at his word and, using connections he'd made through his investigator's work, got a job with the Harris County prosecutor and moved to Houston. And there, working a full forty hours a week, Linebarger enrolled at South Texas College of Law, the same school that spawned David Graham's lawyer, Dan Cogdell. Four years later Linebarger passed the bar and returned to Fort Worth, where, true to his word, Tim Curry hired Linebarger as an assistant D.A. In another half dozen years he was out on his own as a defense lawyer, and has made his reputation in major drug cases in federal court. Prior to the Graham-

Zamora case, Linebarger has never represented a murder defendant, and his drug defense practice is lucrative enough that he certainly doesn't need the money.

When asked about Diane Zamora, Linebarger becomes very serious. "I am telling you, and I can't say this often enough, she is no killer. I don't profess to have all the answers, what went wrong and all that, but my heart goes out to this little girl. She is no killer, period."

Odd as it may seem, defending Diane on murder charges is a bigger problem than defending David Graham. The state has already elected to try the teen lovers separately, and since Diane is first on the firing line, a rather tricky quirk in the law comes into play. Under the hearsay rule, even if David's confession is admitted in his trial, it's inadmissible against Diane unless he testifies against her. The same holds true with Diane's confession; her statements can't be used to convict David unless she takes the stand against him.

In ninety-nine percent of criminal cases involving multiple defendants, lawyers adhere to the first-guy-to-stool-off principle. That is, the first defendant to inform on the other gets less time—sometimes complete immunity—in jail. Diane and David thus far have made the offering of a decent plea bargain impossible. They continue to vow their love in spite of everything, each flatly refusing to consider testifying against the other, and continue to write corny love letters to each other in spite of their lawyers' advice to the contrary.

Should either defendant decide that their passion will not survive a lifetime of incarceration in separate prisons, there is a multitude of choices each could make. The charges currently stand at capital murder (in other states it's known as murder one), which the state will likely have a tough time proving to begin with. Capital murder convictions result in only two choices as to sentencing, death by lethal injection or life in prison with no parole eligibility for forty years. In David's and Diane's cases, the state has already announced that it won't seek the death penalty. The prosecution says it's because Adrianne's parents have requested that they not ask for the defendants to die, though there's a suspicion that the D.A.'s staff doesn't feel it could win a death sentence for these two youngsters to begin with. Besides, capital murder charges are a stretch in this case due to the legal requirements to obtain a conviction.

Capital murder under Texas statutes exists only when the victim is a policeman or fireman in the performance of their duties, murder of a child, or commission of a murder while engaged in another felony, such as a rape or robbery. In the Graham-Zamora cases there's a paragraph at the end of the indictment stating that David and

Diane committed murder while engaged in a kidnapping. Kidnapping is a broad statute, but convincing a jury that Adrianne on that fateful night went somewhere she didn't want to go is a task of major proportions.

If the jury doesn't buy the state's capital murder evidence, they can then choose a variety of lesser offenses.

On the next level down from capital murder—and here's where David's and Diane's convictions will more than likely fall—the offense becomes a class-A felony, with penalties ranging from five to ninety-nine years of life in prison. With such a broad range in punishment options, the first defendant to cut a deal with the D.A. could benefit greatly.

In discussing possible plea agreements, Linebarger puts it this way: "The publicity is killing us. With all the ink the case is getting, the D.A.'s office can't fade the criticism they'd get for coming up with an offer we could live with. Without the TV and newspaper coverage we might get justice in this case. But now, hell no."

The prosecution's activities thus far bear Linebarger out in this statement. The district attorney made David Graham an offer of a class-A felony life sentence in return for a guilty plea. The class-A felony, however, would be an aggravated offense—which designates crimes committed with a deadly weapon—meaning that David

would have to serve thirty-five years before possibility of parole. Since David would be eligible
for parole in *forty* years even if he's convicted of
capital murder, the D.A.'s offer amounts to only a
five-year reduction. Dan Cogdell turned the deal
down flat.

Unless Diane cuts a deal, she's more difficult to
defend because there's no question of admitting
her confession. Before they ever called in the
stenographer, Grand Prairie police read Diane
her rights and had her sign a waiver of counsel.
Once that's done, no amount of trickery on the
part of detectives voids a statement that the suspect might give. Additionally, prosecutors have
statements from Jay Guild—who is no longer at
the Naval Academy but who will appear as a
state's witness against Diane—and Sandra
Trevino, the high school chum who lived down
the street from the Zamoras, as corroborating evidence to the confession.

Because his client is in serious trouble as far as
evidence is concerned, John Linebarger—assisted
ably by Mike Androvet, the media consultant—
has taken a public-relations approach to Diane's
defense, and it's a very effective campaign. She
has come to court for various hearings and
arraignments in a series of attractive, modest
dresses, and she makes a good impression. Trim
and petite, she walks in from the holding cell
with her gaze down in a humble attitude, and sits

at the defense table in an attentive yet demure posture. She seems at all times to be tiny, all alone, and bewildered at the circumstances in which she finds herself. To look at Diane in her present state is heartbreaking, and the effect of her appearance on a jury—particularly if there's a mother or two on the panel—could be a factor.

Additionally, Linebarger and Androvet have fed the media's hunger for pictorial records of the case. With Diane Zamora, there simply are no pictures available to the press other than her mug shot, which is a public record. When Diane was arrested, the case had not drawn national attention as yet, so there were no cameramen on the scene to snap her photo as she entered the jail.

So there are no pictures except for the albums full of Diane's photos that remain the property of the Zamora family. Early on in the case, Androvet's office took charge of all of Carlos and Gloria's pictures of their daughter and the dispensing of same, which places Androvet in the unique position of being able to control Diane's image as seen in the public eye. And Androvet has done an excellent job in this regard. Every photo of Diane that has appeared in magazines or newspapers shows her at her best, with David at the prom or military ball, or pristine in her white Naval Academy uniform, or gazing wistfully into the distance during her senior picture shoot taken at Marcel's Studios in Fort Worth.

There was a major glitch, however. When *People* magazine came calling, Androvet furnished the magazine's representatives with a raft of photos for publication, which *People* snapped up. The magazine hit the newsstands with Adrianne's glamour shot prominently on the cover (incidentally, this was *People*'s best-selling issue of 1996). Yet in spite of assurances by the magazine's reps, there, alongside all the prom and Naval Academy pictures, was Diane's mug shot. Understandably, Androvet hit the ceiling, and any photos furnished by the Zamoras since then have been accompanied by stern warnings as to the lawsuit that will likely result should the newspaper or magazine violate the (now written) agreement not to publish pictures of Diane in custody.

Androvet has also orchestrated a series of press releases. During the first week in February, for example, when Diane celebrated her nineteenth birthday while in the county jail, the newspapers suddenly had a scoop that listed the items she'd requested as presents. These were: a twelve-dollar Walkman tape player from the jail commissary along with several tapes, not by Collective Soul or Stone Temple Pilots, but readings of classical novels so that Diane can continue her education while incarcerated. Such tidbits sprinkled around the media help improve

Diane's image, and more than anything else right now, image improvement is what she needs.

In spite of the evidence against his client, Linebarger does have some ammunition to use in the trial. The confessions given by the lovebirds reek of conspiracy. It's almost as if Diane and David got their stories straight in order to share equal blame for the crime. Linebarger will get all the mileage he can out of the allegation that Diane was so dependent on David that she'd say anything he asked. The jury will have plenty of food for thought in this regard; even the police lab acknowledges that the blow which crushed Adrianne's skull more than likely came from the left. Anyone can see that Diane is incapable of picking up a twenty-five-pound weight with her mangled left hand, much less crashing the weight down on another person's head from behind. So at trial, regardless of the confession, Linebarger will assert that Diane wasn't telling the truth, that David inflicted both the blow to the head and the gunshot wounds, and that Diane's passion for David has caused her to accept partial blame. (David's camp, of course—should David's confession be admitted—will take the opposite stand.)

One major loss for the prosecution case is the murder vehicle. Subsequent to Adrianne Jones's murder the Mazda in question suffered repossession. After the Zamoras surrendered the Mazda, the lot's owner sold the vehicle to a number of other persons before the cops tracked the Mazda down. Before the car—along with the blood the lab will have found inside—can come into evidence, there must be a series of chain-of-custody witnesses to detail where the vehicle has been. If even one of the renters isn't available to testify, then the state won't be able to present any evidence in connection with the auto.

None of which gets around the fact that Diane has confessed her involvement in the murder. Linebarger's best shot is to convince her to testify against David. If so, he would find the district attorney's office more than willing to listen. Defense attorneys aren't the only ones who can analyze a confession's defects, and the state has a few capable lawyers on its payroll to give a neutral appraisal of the situation. And scoff though they might in public and in press conferences, prosecutors can't help but frown a bit when they look at what happened up in Colorado, particularly with Cogdell pouring coals on the fire at every opportunity. So while the state must consider Diane Zamora's conviction practically a given, the same doesn't hold true with the case against David Graham. Ergo, in any sort of plea negotiation, Diane holds most of the cards.

In the meantime, however, Diane and David continue to write love letters back and forth— which jail personnel read at length, Xerox a copy for the D.A.'s files, and then leak the juicier portions to the media—and vow to be true to each other until their dying days. Newspapers have done their best to instill something sinister into the letters' contents, and have stated that Diane's and David's devotion to each other indicates lack of remorse for their crime, but most observers feel that the only thing that the love letters show is how moonstruck adolescents can be.

Linebarger, incidentally, has shown a devotion to his client far above the call of duty. His original retainer came from Miguel Mendoza along with others of Diane's relatives, and pass-the-hat contributions from the faithful at El Templo. The money ran out in January, and though the court has now appointed Linebarger to the case at county expense, appointment fees amount to a pittance. Linebarger continues to believe that his client is no killer, and for the duration of this case, she will not lack for legal counsel.

The Tarrant County assistant district attorney who would most like to hear from Diane Zamora is named Mike Parrish. He's one step down from chief assistant Allan Levy, and he's the head prosecutor in the case. Parrish is a partially bald, square-jawed man who looks a decade younger than his fifty years, and he's been around awhile. He and John Linebarger once prosecuted cases together when Linebarger was a member of the

D.A.'s staff, and like him, Parrish also worked his way up from a police beat.

From Dallas, he put in his application with the DPD soon after graduating from high school. Because of the Vietnam War, the lack of available manpower caused the Dallas Police, along with most of the major departments in the country, to lower their hiring eligibility age from twenty-one to eighteen. Parrish's graduating class from the police academy became known as the Kiddie Cops.

One night after Parrish had been with the force for three years, he and his partner responded to an officer-down emergency call near the corner of Bryan Street and Fitzhugh Avenue, which was and still is in one of the nastier Dallas neighborhoods. Their siren wailing full-blast, the officers sped east down Bryan Street in front of Hispanic beer joints with names such as the Rocket Lounge and the Astro Club at speeds ranging from sixty to eighty miles an hour. In the middle of the Fitzhugh Avenue intersection they collided with a northbound police vehicle responding to the same emergency call. The vehicles were total wrecks; three policemen, Parrish included, required extensive hospitalization as a result of the accident, and the fourth officer died at the scene.

"It was all about the sirens," Parrish says in his office, on the eleventh floor of the Tarrant County

Justice Center, "and accidents like what we had is the reason police sirens pulsate today, and that's the truth. See, with those beer joints on both sides of the street and tall hedges at the corner, it was impossible for us to see the other squad car, and since both out sirens, ours and the other car's, were making exactly the same sounds on the same frequency, we couldn't hear them as long as our own siren was going. Now today, police sirens run on one short note followed by a second note of a different wavelength, and the reason for that is so that two police cars speeding to the same scene can hear each other. Back in those days we couldn't hear each other, and we busted our butts."

Parrish permanently injured his neck and was off the job for a year after the accident. During his enforced break he took advantage of a police incentive program by enrolling at Southern Methodist University. Even after his return to duty—office duty, he still wasn't physically fit to patrol in a squad car—he continued his college work, and received his bachelor's degree from SMU while still running a desk for DPD.

"It was obvious after the wreck," Parrish says, "that the police job wasn't going to take me anywhere. Where it's at in being a cop is on the streets. Office work with the police department is just like any other government job, filling out form after form after form. Seven years after the accident I still couldn't get clearance to return to patrol duty, so finally I asked the department to put me on disability retirement. They granted it, too, and it turned out to be the luckiest break of my life. I used my retirement income to pay my way through law school, and here I am."

Parrish attended law school at Texas Tech in Lubbock, and upon passing the bar he considered only two jobs, both as prosecutors, one in Dallas County and the other in Tarrant. He's been with the Tarrant County District Attorney for twenty years.

"Private practice, yeah, I could do that," Parrish says. "A lot of people do. But a lot of people don't have the obligations I've got." He points to a photo of his children on his credenza. "People do what they do," Parrish says, "and this is my bag here. Occasionally you get some satisfaction out of knowing you're performing a service in prosecuting these people. And satisfaction's as good as money at times. It's what I do. It's what I'll always do."

When Parrish drew the assignment to prosecute Graham and Zamora, he picked Michelle Hartman as his second chair in the case. Like most ADA's, she has plenty of other things to do. While her superior in Graham-Zamora has shoved other matters aside to concentrate on the case at hand, Hartman continues to be assigned full-time to a felony court, a load that included over a hundred files.

"Right there," she says, tilting her chair and pointing to a rack of folders on an upright file case behind her desk. "It's just mind-boggling, and I don't have time to turn around."

"How do you handle the media pressure?" the interviewer says.

"I don't. I don't have time to talk to those people. Mr. Parrish does all that with the newspapers. I do some research on the case, but until the trial is actually happening, I'm more involved with my other stuff." Hartman never refers to Parrish by his first name. She's only a couple of years removed from law school, this is her first case in the media spotlight, and she's a bit wide-eyed over it all.

Michelle Hartman is from Houston, where her father is an ADA. He was the chief prosecutor in a high-profile case wherein the daughter of a prominent Houston attorney had her mother and father killed; the case was the subject of Clifford Irving's excellent book entitled *Daddy's Girl*, and also the subject of Jack Olsen's *Cold Kill.*

Did watching her father work cause Michelle to want to grow up and put the bad guys away?

"Nah." She brushes this off. "I wanted to dance. All I did since I was six years old, and all I ever wanted to do."

It was her love of the dance that brought her to

Fort Worth in the first place, since TCU boasts one of the finer performing-arts curriculums in the country. She stuck with dancing until the second semester of her junior year.

"It was really sort of disheartening," she says, "to see all these people who are excellent dancers, really artists, but are starving to death. I just didn't want to die as an old gypsy or something [gypsies are Broadway dancers who move from show to show and audition to audition], so I decided I'd better get into something to put food on the table."

Hartman's undergraduate grades were excellent, though her major was about as far removed from the practice of law as a course of study can be, so she gained acceptance to the law school at St. Mary's University in San Antonio. She passed the bar in 1993, came to the Tarrant County D.A.'s office, and continues to labor in the D.A.'s trenches to this day.

When asked about any details regarding the Graham-Zamora prosecution, Hartman is brief and to the point. "Look, anything about that, ask Mr. Parrish. We're worried about the judge issuing a gag order as it is, and I don't really know what I'm supposed to say and what I'm not supposed to say. It's Mr. Parrish's case, really, so talk to him."

There is one sure way to get a rise out of Michelle Hartman regarding the Graham-

Zamora prosecution, and that's to mention Dan Cogdell's name. When asked to comment on some matter on which Cogdell is quoted in the paper, Hartman bristles. "Oh? I haven't read about that. What's he saying now?" she says, pronouncing "he" as if she's saying, that s.o.b. who's so in love with himself. Hartman and Cogdell have already clashed in pretrial matters, and if the two should lock horns in the courtroom once the trial gets underway, fans of Court TV should expect some fur to fly.

David's fate regarding admissibility of his murder confession rests with the trial judge, and Joe Drago is a hard individual to read. He's been on the bench for twelve years, which translates to three elected terms of office. He's a switchover Republican, having run on the GOP ticket in the last election. Drago is also a former Tarrant County prosecutor with no experience on the defense side. This normally describes a judge who will rule on all major issues in the prosecution's favor, and let the defense appeal his decisions if the defense attorneys so desire. In the Graham-Zamora case, however, Drago's performance thus far has been neutral.

For example, in a recent hearing John Linebarger petitioned Drago for a restraining order. Specifically, Linebarger wanted to prevent the local NBC affiliate, Channel 5, from airing the

NBC television movie *Love's Deadly Triangle: The Texas Cadet Murder Case* in the Dallas-Fort Worth area because of the movie's possible effect in poisoning the jury pool before the trial. The judge asked Tarrant County for permission to hire a legal expert to research the laws regarding decisions of this nature, and listened attentively to witnesses both from Linebarger's side and the lawyers representing the television station. In the end, Drago's legal counsel informed him that he was powerless to stop airing of the movie, but Drago's decision contained some strong words for the TV station. He said in no uncertain terms that although he couldn't grant the restraining order, he believed very strongly that airing of the movie would poison the jury pool, and that he would be obliged if Channel 5 would refrain from showing the movie on its own. Channel 5 did in fact choose not to show the picture in the DFW viewing area.

Nonetheless, Texas judges are one hundred percent political animals, and Texas is a state where just about every politician runs on a platform of being tough on crime. Judge Drago is no exception to this rule. In a high-profile case such as Graham-Zamora, should the judge throw out David's confession and let a defendant walk on such a heinous offense, then the jurist's opponent would be certain to use this ruling against the judge in the next election, and Judge Drago must keep such issues in mind when rendering decisions.

For a preview of the type of decisions we can expect from the bench once Graham-Zamora goes to trial, it might behoove us to hark back to a hearing held in early December when Dan Cogdell petitioned for a reduction in David's bail. Ever since his arrest he'd been held under a $250,000 bond, which Janice and Jerry Graham cannot afford to post. Texas law is very clear with regard to bail for criminal defendants; if one is held for a period of sixty days under bond that one is unable to post, then one is entitled to a reduction hearing. Absent a showing by the prosecution that the defendant is a risk to flee jurisdiction once he or she is out of jail, then the court is required to reduce bail to an affordable level. In a hearing before the bench, the judge becomes the jury as well, meaning that the judge can weigh the evidence and assign credibility to all witnesses.

The hearing began with Cogdell putting on a bail bondsman who testified that he'd investigated the Graham family finances, and that in his opinion the Grahams could afford to post bond somewhere in the neighborhood of fifty thousand dollars. The bail bondsman, Ronnie Long, had been operating in Tarrant County for twenty years, and since he had no stake in the case other than to collect a bond fee should David be granted lower bail, one must assume that his testimony was accurate. Having presented this evidence, Cogdell then rested, and the state began its presentation of evidence that David was a risk to flee. Mike Parrish did the honors on behalf of the People of Texas.

Parrish first called as witnesses Gary Lynn Foster and Steve Noonkester. Foster testified that he'd indeed found Adrianne's body on his property, and the Mansfield policeman stated that he'd indeed later viewed the body at the Tarrant County Morgue. Both witnesses also identified the grisly crime-scene photos of Adrianne as being the body they'd seen. This testimony was necessary in order to establish that the crime had indeed been committed. Evidence of the crime was already before the court, having been placed there at David's initial bond hearing, so it's assumed that the current testimony was in the nature of refreshing the judge's memory.

After Noonkester left the stand, Parrish then addressed the bench. "Our next witness is in another courtroom, Your Honor. We'd like to ask for a recess until we can produce the witness."

Drago then called a fifteen-minute recess, during which there was a lot of speculation as to the next witness's identity. Since Parrish had indicated that the witness was in another court, the assumption was that the witness was either a lawyer or perhaps a detective who was testifying in another case on the state's behalf. After the allotted quarter hour had passed, one and all resumed their seats in the courtroom.

Judge Drago waited on the bench expectantly, but no witness had yet appeared. Parrish stood at the prosecution table, clearing his throat, shuffling his feet. Judge Drago lifted his eyebrows. Parrish uttered an inaudible sigh of relief as, finally, the witness clanked in.

And "clank" is the proper word for it. The man who entered from the same holding cell where David had emerged at the start of the hearing was a blocky and deep-chested Anglo with a full head of coal black hair. His prisoner's jumpsuit was a couple of sizes too small, thus restricting his movements, and he was having difficulty in walking because of the leg irons shackled around his ankles. There was a momentary feeling within the courtroom that a mistake had been made, but the witness quickly dispelled all doubt by approaching the court clerk and raising his hand for swearing in.

Once sworn, the witness ascended to the box with a rattle of chains, sat down with his gaze darting back and forth, and started visibly as Parrish opened the questioning.

"Please state your full name for the record," Parrish said.

The witness seemed uncertain. "Carl Don

Martin," he finally said. His voice was high, his accent from one of our rural communities.

"And where do you reside?"

"Well, I'm in the county jail right now."

Parrish seemed dissatisfied with the answer. "Well, where do you *normally* reside, Mr. Martin?"

"Oh." Martin showed his version of a disarming grin. "Pauls Valley, Oklahoma."

Parrish resumed his seat at the table and folded his hands. "And are you acquainted with the defendant in this case, David Christopher Graham?"

"Oh, yeah. I know him, all right." Martin failed to so much as glance in David's direction.

"And how did you become acquainted with Mr. Graham?" Parrish said.

"They brung him into the cell with me."

"At the jail?"

"Yes sir."

"You were cell mates, then?"

"For a time we was."

"And during the time while you celled with Mr. Graham, did you have occasion to discuss the charges against him?"

"Oh, yeah," Martin said. "We talked about every day."

"And was there an occasion," Parrish said, "when you and Mr. Graham discussed his possible release on bail?"

"Sure was." Martin showed another grin, this one of the hopeful variety.

"Where and when did this conversation occur?"

"Was on a Tuesday, I think. We was in the day-room."

"The dayroom being a common area to all cells in the cell block?" Parrish seemed well acquaint-ed with the county jail facilities.

"Yes sir. Where the television's at."

"I see," Parrish said. "At that time, did Mr. Graham discuss his plans with you if he should be released on bail?"

"Yes sir. He tole me he was gonna get a gun, and that nobody around here was ever gonna see him again."

Parrish paused for the testimony to sink in, then said, "He said he'd get a gun?"

"Yes sir."

"And that he would leave the community?"

"Yes sir."

"And that no one in the community would ever see him again?"

"That's what he said," Martin answered.

Parrish shuffled papers. He'd met the state's burden; evidence of David's planned flight was admissible in this hearing regardless of the source, and it was not the court's job, after per-mitting Cogdell to cross-examine, to weigh the evidence and determine the witness's credibility, such as it was. "Pass the witness, Your Honor," Parrish finally said.

Judge Drago showed very little emotion, and now turned to the defense table. "Cross, Mr. Cogdell?" the jurist said.

Cogdell had been watching the proceedings with his jaw slack, and now closed his mouth with an audible click of his teeth. "Mr. . . . Martin, is it?"

"Carl Don Martin, yes sir." Martin seemed a bit miffed, as if the defense attorney should have been paying better attention.

"Mr. Martin, what are you in jail for?"

The witness seemed hesitant, and looked at the prosecution table. No help there. Finally he said, "I'm not convicted of anything."

"I didn't ask that, sir," Cogdell said. "What is it that they're *saying* you did?"

"Well, the charges are, attempted capital murder."

"Okay. Who is it they're saying you tried to kill, Mr. Martin?"

"Was a River Oaks policeman, but I—"

"I see," Cogdell said. "And what is the amount of your bail?"

Martin seemed as if he might have developed a frog in his throat. "Hundred thousand."

"A hundred thousand dollars." Cogdell slowly shook his head. "Is this your first time in jail, sir?"

Martin assumed a hangdog look. "No." He

looked to the spectators section, where a gentleman in a suit had taken a seat while the testimony was in progress. This man, it would turn out, was the witness's attorney, there to make certain that his client said nothing to injure defense against his own charges.

"Well," Cogdell said, "how many other times have you been in jail, sir?"

Here the witness became uncooperative, and Cogdell painstakingly dragged out of Mr. Martin that in addition to the attempted capital charge, he'd done time for burglary along with three other felonies, and that he was in leg irons in the courtroom because he'd once escaped from jail and was considered a flight risk. Cogdell was doing his best to maintain his composure, but a hint of sarcasm kept creeping into his tone.

Mr. Martin's criminal record now exposed for one and all, Cogdell said, "So obviously you've been around the system a time or two, and as an experienced jail resident you'd know that the district attorney tends to make deals with people that help them out, wouldn't you?"

Martin looked a bit sheepish. "They hadn't offered me nothing."

"So you're just up here telling this to be a good citizen, right?"

Martin was uncertain. "I'm not—"

"Doing your duty," Cogdell said. "Tell me

something. When did Mr. Parrish over there"—he pointed at the prosecution table—"first approach you and ask you about Mr. Graham's jail conversations with you?"

Martin looked totally puzzled.

"Well," Cogdell said, "were the two of you out to lunch over at the Bar Association, or—"

"Objection." Parrish came halfway out of his chair. Judge Drago sustained. Cogdell was out of line and obviously knew it, took a moment to regroup, and plunged ahead.

"Mr. Martin," Cogdell said, "Mr. Parrish didn't approach you at all, did he?"

"Well, naw," the witness replied. "I guess he really didn't."

"You approached him, didn't you?"

"Suppose I did," the witness admitted. He crossed his legs, and the chain on his leg irons rattled.

"Well, how did you do that? Call him on the phone, or . . . ?"

"I wrote him a letter," Martin said.

"Mmm-hmm." Cogdell looked to the bench. "Request production of the letter, Your Honor."

The defense was entitled to see the document, and this caused a rummaging around at the prosecution table. Finally Parrish confessed apologetically that he'd left the witness's contact letter in his office. Judge Drago ordered another recess so that Parrish could come up with the letter. After the pause, Parrish turned the letter over to Cogdell and the judge called order. The letter was written on yellow legal pad paper in a tiny cursive scrawl.

Cogdell looked the document over for a long time. The message was quite lengthy, and described how David had told Martin in his cell that he and Diane had murdered Adrianne Jones. There was no mention in the letter of the conversation regarding David's plan to jump bail. Cogdell finished reading, stared at the signature on the letter, and sat upright, rattling the letter in the direction of the witness box.

"I'm missing something here," Cogdell said. "Haven't you testified that your name is Martin?"

"Yes sir, Carl Don Martin," the witness said. "That's me, all right."

ADA Parrish coughed off to one side and appeared slightly red-faced.

"Well, is that the name of the person signing this letter?" Cogdell said.

The witness reacted as if a lightbulb had exploded inside his head. "Oh, that. Well, I can explain—"

"Yeah, please do," Cogdell said. "Please explain to the court why you wrote a letter to the prosecutor, Mr. Parrish, over there, and signed the letter Jerry Clark if your name is really Carl Don Martin."

The witness's answer was accompanied by a

few titters from the spectators section. "Jerry Clark," the witness said, "that's the name I was arrested under."

"Don't you mean," Cogdell said, "that Jerry Clark is the name you furnished the officer upon your arrest?"

"Well, yeah," the witness replied. "I suppose I did."

"So when the police got you to jail, they wouldn't find out about your record, right? I'll withdraw that question, I think we already know. Okay, Mr. Clark, or Mr. Martin, or whatever your name is," Cogdell said, "is it still your testimony that you're up here just to do the right thing, and that the prosecution hasn't offered any reduction in the charges against you in return for your testimony here today?"

Martin seemed to think it over. "Not just for today," he finally said.

"Oh," Cogdell said, "You mean, you're supposed to be on ready alert for the duration of Mr. Graham's trial, is that right?"

"Well . . ." The witness looked to Parrish, who was suddenly very interested in something in the far corner of the room. "Something like that, I guess," the witness finally said.

"So," Cogdell said, "exactly what have you been promised for your testimony?"

"Nothing firm."

"Just that you'd talk about it, depending on how your testimony worked out?"

The witness studied the floor. "Something like that," he said.

Cogdell dropped the letter in obvious disgust. "No further questions, Your Honor."

The foregoing is paraphrased, mainly because Cogdell's cross-examination of Mr. Carl Don Martin, a.k.a. Jerry Clark, lasted for a couple of hours, but the condensed version pretty well describes what went on during David's bail-reduction hearing. Judge Drago put off his decision on the matter until the following day.

Apparently Judge Drago found Mr. Martin/ Clark to be quite believable, because the following day he entered an order that refused David's request for a reduction in bail. The point here is not to criticize the decision to keep David incarcerated, as none of us like to consider the consequences of a young man who's confessed to such a hideous crime walking around free on bond. The point is, however, to illustrate the options available to the court, if it so chooses, to adjust the law in order to fit the court's perception of what's good for the public.

This example is a roundabout way of getting to the main issue, which is the admissibility at trial of David's confession, which will also be up to Judge Drago. It seems, particularly with the amount of media coverage connected to this case, that the judge will not be swayed by legal niceties. David confessed to a grisly murder. If Diane does decide to testify for the state, then the prosecution won't necessarily need David's confession in order to get a conviction. Under that set of circumstances, David's confession may well go out the window. But if Diane remains steadfast in her death-do-us-part position, then David's confession will almost certainly be admitted, whether the law was twisted a bit to obtain it or not. The defense will then have the avenue of appeal open to them, of course, but appellate courts, in high-profile cases, usually back the trial court's actions no matter what the trial court decides.

# Epilogue

Ever since the media vultures descended to pick poor Adrianne's bones during the first week in September 1996, life for Roy and Linda Jones has returned to being a living hell. Just as they'd learned to cope with the loss of their daughter and get on with their lives, the press dredged up all the horrible memories all over for them. The volume of calls at all hours of the day and night caused them to have their phone number changed and unlisted. Reporters have hung out a block from Mansfield High School, stopping students on their way home to ask questions about Adrianne's sexual habits, some even offering money for the slightest juicy tidbit. To the high schoolers' credit, for the most part they haven't taken the bait, and have dutifully reported to Roy and Linda what was going on.

Linda's reaction to the barrage has come under criticism in some corners, because she's accepted some of the calls and agreed to appear on some of the sleazier talk shows, all in an attempt to do something to cleanse her daughter's memory. Remember that this is a small-town lady without the smarts of the more hip among us—just the type, in fact, on whom the Jerry Springers of the world so love to prey. To Linda, an appearance on Maury Povich, for example, seems no different than an interview on *Nightline* with Ted Koppel. And once you've gone before the cameras, you have no protection from personal questions from the studio audience, most of whose main interest is in finding out whether your horribly murdered daughter was sleeping around.

In doing research for this book and gradually forming my personal opinion that David was lying to Diane when he told her that he had sex with Adrianne Jones, I had conversations both in person and over the phone with any number of people. These included some kids who'd been on the cross-country trip in question, and one memorable lunch with three young men on Christmas break from their Doolie year at the Air Force Academy. The talk with these cadets was probably the biggest eye-opener during the entire research process. Apparently David developed a reputation during induction summer as not only being gung-ho Air Force but an individual given to making up stories. These boys gave several examples of stories David told during nighttime bull sessions that turned out not to be true. This got me to wondering, and also to looking at my research from an entirely different perspective.

At any rate, once I'd formed my opinion, I took the opportunity to bounce my theory off of some of my adult friends. The reactions I got were pretty surprising. These reactions ranged from total disbelief (as in the case of the secretary to a lawyer friend of mine who opined that David's story must be the gospel because she'd *read it in the newspaper*) to powerful skepticism, but the general consensus was that my opinion was full of hockey pucks. Of great interest were the number of people, most of them women, who thought that the tale of sexual conquest must be true because if it wasn't, why would Adrianne have agreed to go out with David on the night of the murder to begin with?

That such questions would come from females indicates to me the full circle to which we've come in moral evaluation over the past forty years or so. Think about what you're asking, ladies: *If she'd never been to bed with the guy, why would she agree to go out with him?* No one knows, other than David, what story he used to lure Adrianne out of the house that night, but the answer could be any number of things. I'm fairly certain at this point that the date came as a result of a phone call that David placed to the Golden Chicken on the afternoon of Adrianne's death. For her, after midnight, when her folks were in bed, was the time of her regular social activities. David wasn't a stranger to Adrianne—though most considered them no more than passing acquaintances—and it could very well be that he asked her for a date ("Hi, this is David from cross-country, remember me?") and that she accepted, just as she'd done any number of other times. The fact that she sneaked out of the house to go with him might mean no more than if he'd showed up at her door at eight p.m. to go to the movies. The sneaking out business was merely Adrianne's normal method of doing things.

Whether David and Adrianne had engaged in sex previously has no bearing on the crime, of course—Diane believed that they had regardless of whether the story is true. Yet there's something in these kids' confessions that offers more food for thought on this issue. Both David and Diane agree that Adrianne, when confronted by Diane over having sex with Diane's boyfriend, physically attacked David in the car's front seat, and that Diane swung the dumbbell weight, in part, because she wanted to protect David from harm. The question is, why would Adrianne lash out at David? One explanation is that she was angry because David had betrayed their secret and set her up for a confrontation, but it's just as plausible that she was angry because he'd been spreading lies about her.

NBC and the producers of *Love's Deadly*

*Triangle: The Texas Cadet Murder Case* want to believe David's story verbatim, because it gives them the opportunity to show an extended sex scene in their movie. Conversely, I very much want to believe that David is lying, because if he is, it gives Roy and Linda Jones some relief from having to offer explanations about their murdered little girl's sexual behavior. This child is dead, and if we must give benefit of doubt, let's allow Adrianne to rest in peace.

Writing a book about a murder case that has yet to come to trial is a touchy proposition for a number of reasons, not the least of which is the effect the book can have on the trial itself. With that in mind I've given pseudonyms to quite a few persons described and quoted in this book. For example, anyone who is a potential witness—and who has yet to appear on the witness stand in preliminary matters, as is the case with Gary Lynn Foster (his real name), the man who found Adrianne's body on his land—is entitled to privacy and is identified herein under an assumed name. I've made three notable exceptions in Jay Guild, the young man who befriended Diane at Annapolis, and Mandy Gotch and Jenifer Kearney, the roommates who took Diane's story to the chaplain, because these individuals have been pictured and widely discussed in newspapers and national magazines.

Additionally, I've used pseudonyms when my source was legally a minor child, even though some of these kids were chomping at the bit to be mentioned in a publication that they could show to their friends. This is also true with the youngster identified as James Drummond, even though his real name has been prominently featured in local newspapers and at least one national magazine.

As to members of the 1996–97 Naval Academy plebe class and the 1996–97 Doolie class at the Air Force Academy with whom I've had contact, I've left their identities out altogether at their request, because according to them they've received strong suggestions from academy officials not to discuss the Graham-Zamora case with anyone. In connection with the foregoing statement, I will state further that David's roommate at the Academy was named Bryan Denaro, and that I've had no contact with him.

As for other persons who have given me information or much appreciated encouragement on this project, I offer heartfelt thanks to the following and apologize to those whose names I might inadvertently omit:

Dan Cogdell, Rob Swofford, John Linebarger, Mike Androvet, Mike Parrish, Michelle Hartman, these the lawyers, and

Mike Cochran, Skip Hollandsworth, Carlton

Stowers, Pete Slover, Tim Madigan, these the newsguys, and

Lieutenant Commander Patrick McCarthy at the United States Naval Academy and

Master Sergeant Ampule at the United States Air Force Academy, and

Lieutenant Junior Grade James Ewen Hail, Annapolis Class of 1994, for the Plebe Summer information, and

Gary Layman with the National Security Agency, for information concerning the Office of Special Investigations, and

Patrick Gill of the Civil Air Patrol, and

Deputy Chief Geary of the Grand Prairie P.D., and

Dominick Abel, my agent, who, after twelve long years, continues to put up with me, for what reason God only knows, and

Michaela Hamilton, my editor who, once this is all put to bed, will likely sleep for a week, and

Daniel, John, Sarah, and Gregory Gray, my children, who if I didn't love so doggone much I never would have gotten into this project, and

Martha Crosland Gray, my wife, my life, my everlasting love.